WITH INTENT

On a bitterly cold winter's night, a policeman approaches the driver of a car that has stalled in a dingy back street, and is shot in the face. The detectives who hunt for the gunman are faced by an almost insoluble problem, for the crime seems motiveless.

When, through sheer dogged determination, they eventually get to their man they are unable to bring him to trial. What can they do if there is insufficient evidence? What should be done, if anything, about criminals whose guilt is known but whom the law cannot touch?

WITH INTENT

Laurence Henderson

First published 1968
by
George G. Harrap & Co. Ltd.

This edition 2001 by Chivers Press
published by arrangement with
the author

FOR OLD AUD

ISBN 0 7540 8594 5

British Library Cataloguing in Publication Data available

Printed and bound in Great Britain by
Bookcraft, Midsomer Norton, Somerset

1

AT 2 A.M. Constable Toms became very conscious that his feet were freezing cold. The biting wind that came up from the railway-line and blew across the waste-land that bordered the footbridge over the line bit through his heavy serge uniform, and swept past him into the empty, frost-rimed streets beyond. It was the time of desolation, the nadir of the night.

Toms had known that this moment was coming since he had come on duty. It had been there before, when he had eaten his supper in the kitchen of his little house. Flushed from the heat of the coke-boiler at his back, his stomach heavy with fried bread and tomatoes, he was luxuriating over his final cup of tea and cigarette when he heard the weather announcement from the television set in the next room. Sleet showers on high ground, gale-force winds in London and the Home Counties, and seven degrees of frost.

Toms had shuddered then. He had come to dread the dragging monotony and bitterness of winter nights at two or three o'clock in the morning, when even the thieves sheltered from the weather in their own beds and he was the only one to walk the streets. It made him feel very alone, and older than his years. He was forty-two now, and no longer ambitious. All his thoughts were centred on getting through the next two years without any real trouble. Then retirement, a quiet job somewhere as a gateman or a storeman, and an end to the lonely walking of hard pavements on bitter nights.

He went slowly past the shuttered shop-fronts and the blank-faced little houses, away from the shrouded bleakness of the railway-line. Selecting the doorway of a small grocery shop, he carefully eased himself into the farthermost corner, as far away from the wind as he could. His fingers were stiff with cold, and it took him some time to search out his tobacco tin from the side-pocket of his tunic. Almost without looking, he rolled himself a thin cigarette, struck a match across his thick, square thumbnail, and drew in the smoke with deep satisfaction.

As he held his cigarette pinched ready for the second drag he heard the car. Almost at once it went past him—a Zodiac, very dirty and without lights. As it passed beneath the street-lamp Toms could see the driver, a small man, hunched so closely over the wheel that only his startling white hair could be seen with any clarity. His driving was ridiculously erratic, veering towards first one kerb and then the other. At the end of the road the car swung wide to negotiate the corner, but instead struck and mounted the kerb with its nearside wheels. The engine coughed and died.

Carefully stubbing his cigarette on the plate-glass window, Toms emerged from his doorway and moved his numbed feet towards the car. He was suddenly glad of something to do, even dealing with a drunk driver. With any luck he might have to take him in to the station.

As he neared the car he slackened his pace. He could see the car very clearly now; he bent his head to read the number-plate—SDE 321D. When he looked up again the driver was no longer crouched over the wheel. He was leaning across to pull down the nearside window. He was smiling, and his hair was no longer white, it was a fine, pale yellow. His face was very young and relaxed. With his left hand he casually stroked a black tube. Toms peered towards him in the long shadows of the street-lamp. He was very close to the car. He cleared his throat. From the car came a curious snicker, and then the whole world split asunder.

To Toms came the conviction that he had been struck by lightning. He clutched desperately at the man, but already he was falling, and his fingers touched only the frozen metal of the car.

6

It was Newcombe, the huge station sergeant, who came out to Toms. He brought with him the newly created Detective Constable Pawson, a tall, dark boy of twenty-four, who sat jammed by Newcombe's eighteen-stone bulk against the passenger door of the old Austin. Several times Pawson cleared his throat, but Newcombe was in no mood for conversation. His massive jaw pointed like the prow of a barge, heavy with outrage.

As they turned into Legume Street Pawson saw the Zodiac with its nearside wheels still perched up on the pavement, the rear window sparkling with diamonds of frost. Then he saw the figure on the pavement: four or five people were grouped round it, and kneeling on the pavement was a very frail-looking figure. Newcombe pulled the car savagely into the kerb, and was out on the road while Pawson was still groping for the door-handle. The figure kneeling beside Toms straightened up: he was a small elderly man, his face pinched with the cold, and a few wisps of grey hair sticking up from his scalp. He clutched a long black overcoat round himself, and Pawson saw with surprise the pyjamas and carpet slippers that showed beneath. Heaped over Toms was a little mound of coats and blankets. As Pawson got out of the car his foot slipped, and, looking down, he saw the blood.

"We didn't like to move him," the little man was saying to Newcombe. "When you don't know exactly what's wrong it can be dangerous, but it is so cold for the poor man."

Newcombe grunted and bent over Toms. He peered very closely, and then he sniffed. Pawson also bent over, and, looking beyond Newcombe's shoulder, suddenly felt very faint as he caught sight of the scorched flesh of what had been Toms's face. He stood transfixed, and then Newcombe mercifully leaned forward to hide it from his view. He swayed at the edge of the kerb, his face covered with an icy sweat, and as he held himself stiffly in a desperate effort to keep from falling the clear, cold air carried to him the sound of the bell of an ambulance from more than a mile away.

2

THE station duty-room was very crowded. Groups of constables from the barracks were mustered: gloved up and mufflered, they waited for instructions. Off-duty C.I.D. and uniformed men were arriving on recall, singly and in pairs. Only Newcombe, still wearing his greatcoat, was moving with any purpose in mind. He shouted into his telephone and glared at his subordinates, all the while constructing a duty rota of the most complex subtlety.

The door of the C.I.D. interview-room opened to emit First Class Detective Sergeant Milton, a sad-eyed, bad-tempered man when, as now, he was called back after three hours' sleep.

"Mr Davies arrived yet, Henry?"

"On his way," said Newcombe. "He's driving himself in, and he wants nothing done till he gets here."

"Any news of Toms?"

"No."

"I'd better keep this joker for Mr Davies then. Give me a shout."

Newcombe grunted and bent over his rota again. He could not see the point of bringing in off-duty men and emptying the police cadet barracks in order to muster a small army. It would have made sense if they had a clear idea of what they were looking for; in the case of a lost child it made sense. In this case it did not—not to Newcombe, but he had his orders, and he was glad of that. Carrying them out gave him something to do.

The hubbub died for a moment, and Newcombe looked up

to see the arrival of Detective Superintendent Harold Davies. He came through the swing doors trailing clouds of tobacco smoke—a large, square man, very much the figure of an artisan, even down to the dilapidated trilby which sat squarely on his head.

He paused as he came level with Newcombe, and jerked his head. Newcombe followed him into his office. Davies did not take off his overcoat; he walked over to sit heavily at his desk.

"You were the first there?"

"Yes, sir."

"Did he say anything?"

"Nothing. He was out, hardly breathing."

"Who is at the hospital?"

"Pawson—I've sent a policewoman, Jenny Hughes, to Toms's wife."

"The car?"

"It's being examined."

"What did you see?"

"Nothing much. I saw Toms, and did what I could. There was a man called Lloyd who did all right. Tried to keep Toms warm, sent for us, and an ambulance. He's in the interview-room with Arthur Milton."

"Have you any ideas?"

"I wish I did."

"What cases has Toms been involved in?"

"Small stuff mostly—drunks, a few fights. I've been checking up trying to think of something myself. The biggest pinch he made was on a break-in, and that was some kids. There's no-one who would set this up for him."

"Someone did."

"Yes."

"What about his home life?"

"Nothing there as far as I know."

"He's got a daughter, hasn't he?"

"She's married, lives up in Rugby somewhere."

"We'll need her smartish if Toms is on the edge."

"I want this feller," said Newcombe.

"We all want him. Let's have this man Lloyd in."

9

Mr Lloyd was no longer wearing his pyjamas, but a long woollen scarf was much in evidence. A small man, his pale bald head had a great frailty under the harsh down-light above the desk, and Davies felt a small shock of surprise that this man among all others should be the one to come forward on a freezing night to comfort a policeman with his face shot away.

Davies got to his feet. "I am Detective Superintendent Davies. Please sit down, Mr Lloyd. I know you want to get back to your home, and I shall try to keep this as short as possible."

"Is there any news of the constable?"

"We're still waiting to hear—he's in the operating theatre now. We don't know what his chances are, but it's thanks to you he's got any chance at all. I've been told that you saw the man. I know you have told your story already, but I would like to hear it from you myself."

"Yes, I understand," said Mr Lloyd.

"Would you like a cigarette?"

"No, thank you. I'll try to be as accurate as I can. It was about half-past two. I'm a very bad sleeper. I heard the constable, as I do on most nights. I felt particularly sorry for him tonight, it was so bitter. I heard him go along the road."

"Which way?"

"North, away from the line; and then some minutes later I heard the car. It made a lot of noise. I heard it screech at the corner, and then there was a bump and it stopped—the engine, I mean. I wondered, of course, whether there had been an accident, but it was all so quiet, and it was such a cold night. Even in my bedroom. . . ."

"What happened next?"

"I heard the constable coming back."

"Was he running?"

"No, he was walking, as before."

"And then?"

"There was the explosion, the shot."

"You knew it was a shot?"

"I guessed; I never thought of it as being anything else."

"Before the shot, did you hear anyone speak? The constable, or the man in the car?"

10

"No, there was nothing. When I heard the shot I got out of bed and went to the window."

"Now," said Davies, "take your time; tell me exactly what you saw when you first looked out of the window."

"The first thing I saw was the car. It was at an angle; the two front wheels were on the pavement, as if the driver had tried to go round the corner too sharply. The driver's door was open, and I saw the back of a man moving away towards the railway-line. The policeman was lying on the pavement; he was very close to the car, not more than a foot away. As mine is the corner house there is a street-lamp almost immediately outside my door. I could see everything on the pavement very clearly."

"Yes?"

"Beyond the road, on the other side of my house, there is only waste-land. It borders the railway line; and there are no lamps. It's in complete darkness unless there's a train passing."

"Did you see this man by the light of a train?"

"No. There's a bridge over the railway line, you reach it by a flight of steps, and at the top is a light so that anyone coming across the bridge can see where the steps are. I heard him walking up the steps, and then he came into the light."

"Did you see his face?"

"No, only his back." Mr Lloyd shut his eyes, tilting his face upward in an agony of concentration. "He was a young man, he walked like a young man. He was taller than me, though not very tall, about five foot nine. He wore a suede jacket with a fur collar, the sort of thing they call a motoring coat."

Davies nodded.

"As he passed directly beneath the lamp I saw that he had white hair."

"You are sure of that?"

"I am. I realize it's important, but I am sure. It was so startling."

"How young would you say this man was?"

"Perhaps twenty or twenty-one, possibly younger."

"What colour was the coat?"

"Dark brown."

"And the fur collar?"

"Grey."

"Did you notice the colour of his trousers?"

"No."

"Were they dark or light?"

"Dark, darkish—it may have been the shadow."

"Did you see any part of his face at all?"

"No, it was curious."

"Curious?"

"He never looked back. He had shot a policeman, left him for dead for all he knew, but he wasn't perturbed. He didn't even glance back to see if anyone was after him. I can't imagine what sort of man he could be."

"Did you see anything else?"

"As he passed under the light I could see he was holding something in his right hand, a sort of stick."

"How long?"

"The part I saw was about eighteen inches. I only saw it for a moment. He was holding it in front of him, and I only saw it when he moved it to one side, adjusting his balance as he took the last step up on to the bridge. It must have been the gun, of course."

"And then?"

"My wife had woken up by then, and one or two other people had come to their windows. I asked my wife to telephone the police and to get an ambulance, then I went out to the constable."

"You did very well, Mr Lloyd."

"It seemed the obvious thing to do."

"You have no doubt that this man had white hair?"

"It's the one thing I have no doubt about. I've even wondered if it could possibly have been a wig or some sort of disguise."

"What makes you think it wasn't?"

"It was too flat—sleek, even—and there was something about this man—it's difficult to describe it—but I don't want to waste your time, I know you only want facts."

"Go on, Mr Lloyd."

12

"He had an air about him—though that's not the word I'm really looking for—but he had this aura about him, a sort of disdain. He didn't seem to care whether he was seen or not; he wasn't in any hurry; he seemed relaxed. He didn't seem frightened or excited. All I'm trying to say is that he wasn't the sort of man who would be interested in disguise. I suppose that sounds a ridiculous thing to say about a man whom I only saw from the back."

"Was there anything else about him that you noticed? Was there anything special about the way he walked?"

"No, there was nothing else."

"I won't keep you any longer, Mr Lloyd. I'm very grateful to you. I know you want to get home to bed. A formal statement can be taken tomorrow. Thank you for what you did."

Davies got up and held out his hand.

"If anything else does occur to you, no matter how trivial, don't think you are wasting my time, get in touch with me at any time. The sergeant will arrange for a car to take you home."

He remained politely standing until Lloyd had closed the door, then he relit his pipe and turned to the window. He wiped condensation from the pane with the back of his hand and stared out into the unbroken blackness of the night. He was aware that in the courtyard below cars were revving up and moving off. He did not look down; the intense blackness held his attention.

3

THE first light of dawn was noted by a very weary George Pawson as he tried to restore the circulation of his cramped legs by massaging the calves. He had now spent almost two hours on the hard wooden bench outside the emergency operating theatre of St Leo's Hospital, waiting for word that Toms could speak to him. Newcombe had given him orders to stick at Toms's side until he either spoke or died, but a very militant Sister had insisted on his leaving. She had been backed up by the house surgeon and Pawson had allowed himself to be moved. He felt a little guilty about this, but was glad that he had not had Mrs Toms to deal with. Poor Jenny Hughes was still at her house. Mrs Toms had collapsed when she had been told, and a local doctor had to be called in to give her a sedative. Jenny Hughes was spending the night with her.

Pawson was tired of smoking cigarettes; he longed for a drink, for some warmth, but, most of all, for something to do. He knew that fifty men had been recalled for duty and were now searching the railway line and the surrounding streets, seeking the gun which might have been thrown away, knocking on doors, asking questions, patiently walking through the bitter cold, quietly controlled, but with a burning determination to find the man who had shot Toms in the face.

Pawson wondered about Toms. He knew very little about him, and had never spoken to him about anything except duty rosters or thieves, but there had been a quality which had caught his respect and affection. He reminded Pawson of his father, who was a cabinet-maker : they both had about them an air of thoughtful consideration and inner calm. It somehow made it even more tragic that he should have been shot down.

The doors of the operating theatre swung open and a very tired house surgeon came out.

Pawson stepped forward.

"There's no point in your going in," said the doctor. "He will be unconscious for some time."

"I have to stay until he comes round, Doctor. If you've no objection I'll wait inside."

The house surgeon made a vague gesture. "Wait until the nurses have made him a little more comfortable; there are some things that have to be done first."

"Is there no news at all, Doctor ?"

"He is very ill, and will be for some time, but the main danger now is shock."

"But he will be all right ?"

"It will take some time to adjust."

"What do you mean ?"

"Look, Sergeant. . . ."

"Constable."

"Constable. You are not a relative, and I must speak to Mr Toms's wife."

"She's under sedation at her home, Doctor. She's taken it very badly."

"Is there no-one else ?"

"A married daughter. We're trying to contact her now, but she's moved up to Rugby."

"I see."

"He's a policeman, Doctor; we worked with him, he's our friend, can't you. . . ?"

"I am sorry . . . both eyes have been so badly damaged that neither will be able to function normally again. They'll probably have to be removed entirely at some time in the future, when Mr Toms has recovered some of his strength."

"I see." A cold sweat broke out along the line of Pawson's spine, and he felt sick.

"You'd better sit down here for a moment."

15

"I'm all right," said Pawson. He brought out his cigarettes again and offered one to the house surgeon. He had some difficulty in striking a match.

"Senseless, isn't it?" said the surgeon; he put his hand on Pawson's shoulder, and then after a moment moved away along the corridor.

Pawson drew very deeply on his cigarette and exhaled a dense cloud of smoke. He watched for some time as it hung lazily in front of the door shielding Toms. Then he moved reluctantly towards the Sister's duty-room to telephone the station.

4

DETECTIVE SERGEANT Arthur Milton passed a weary hand across his eyes, yawned, and glanced at his watch. It showed 5.45. A numbing pressure had begun to build up at the crown of his head. It was a sign he recognized as indication that he had gone too long without sleep, smoked too many cigarettes, and drunk too many cups of metallic-tasting canteen tea. He had studied so many dossiers of unsuccessful criminals that he could no longer comprehend what he saw.

The three hours he had spent on the telephone, wrenched from his night's rest, had achieved two pieces of paper. One listed all known albino criminals—there were three names; the other listed the names of anyone ever arrested by Toms, together with the names of their brothers, fathers, and known friends.

Milton had checked every name on both lists, and on every one he had drawn a blank. In doss-houses, council flats, basements, back-street bedsitters, no-one knew, had heard, had any idea of, a man between eighteen and twenty-six with very pale or white hair, with or without a shotgun.

Milton selected the longest stub in his ashtray and searched his littered desk for matches. He could not find any. He sighed, and thought fleetingly of his wife lying alone in the big bed. He felt very old.

He got up from his desk and went out of the C.I.D. room. The reception area was empty except for the immovable Newcombe. He looked up as Milton came out.

"No?"

Milton shook his head.

"I didn't think he'd be there," said Newcombe. "It was no tea-leaf."

"How do you see this, Henry?"

Newcombe picked up a cigarette packet which had been badly dented, and extracted a few bent cigarettes. "I don't see it. It was no-one from round here, none of the pros. They know we'd put them through a sieve. And, anyway, what would be the point? Toms never put anyone away for more than six months. It wasn't him in particular he was after; he just got in the way."

"That means he's a maniac driving around with this gun ready for anyone who comes."

"He shouldn't be hard to find."

"I'm glad you think so, Henry." Milton took one of the cigarettes and licked the tear in it. "I hate amateurs, they've only got to drop back into their family circle, and there's nothing to look for."

"They can't stop talking."

"Not all of them."

"This one will. If he's not shivering behind the door waiting for us to come for him he'll be thinking he's Billy the Kid, just bursting to tell someone about it."

"Let's hope someone listens to him, then."

"It'll be a bird, sooner or later."

"His mother?"

"Not this one." He lit Milton's cigarette.

"How long did Toms have to go?"

"Two years."

"Poor bastard."

They continued looking at each other across the reception desk, but neither could find words to express what they wanted to say. Eventually Milton nodded, and walked off up the corridor to Davies's room. He knocked, and went in when he heard Davies shout. Inside he immediately felt uncomfortable. Davies always had his office overheated, and now it was acrid with tobacco smoke. Davies was not sitting at his desk. He

18

was standing in front of the large street-map of the Division that was pinned on the side wall to the right of his desk.

"I've finished both lists, sir. There was nothing in either."

Davies nodded, and turned away to his desk.

"Is there any news on the car?"

"Yes." Davies picked up a message pad from his desk. "It belongs to a doctor, and was stolen seven weeks ago from a car-park in Sutton. The plates are false. It's the number of a Morris Minor in Wales, and the licence is a forgery—a good one."

"Professional?"

"The car stalled because the driver didn't change down for the corner."

"He might have been drunk."

"Or a lousy driver."

"It doesn't make sense to have a car duffed up by a pro and driven by a beginner."

"No, it doesn't."

"Did the doctor have anything in the car?"

"Only his gloves; no drugs or anything like that."

Davies sat down heavily in his chair and blew through his pipe, sending up a volcano of ash.

"The worst ones are the ones you can't understand. Of all the coppers in this division Toms is the one who handled himself most like a village bobby. No-one can ever remember him speaking hard to the ones he brought in."

"I know, sir, I've been talking to some of them. If there was anything like a popularity contest for coppers, Toms would have won it."

"I've been looking up his record. Joined when he was nineteen, only had two years for his pension."

"Newcombe was telling me."

"All right," Davies said loudly. "Never mind what we haven't got, let's have a look at what it comes to."

Milton cleared his throat. "Toms was shot, about 2.30 A.M., when he went up to a stalled car at the end of Legume Road. We now know that the car was stolen. The driver was armed, probably with a shotgun, and he used it as soon as Toms

19

approached him. According to Lloyd there was no conversation, the driver made no attempt to talk his way out, and that's unusual for the professional criminal; on the other hand, most amateurs would have tried to run, or tried to keep him back with threats. There was only one man in the car, a young man. No-one saw his face. The only distinguishing feature is his hair. He's not likely to be a known criminal; he probably never saw Toms before, and would have shot anyone who got in his way."

Davies nodded. "That's about it." His telephone rang, and he answered it, listened, and recradled the receiver. He looked reflectively at Milton.

"That was Pawson from the hospital. Toms will live if he comes out of the shock O.K."

Milton's face lightened.

"He's lost both eyes."

"I want this feller," said Milton.

"We all want him."

Milton crushed the end of his cigarette savagely into Davies's ashtray. Davies continued puffing his pipe.

"I was speaking to Mr Miller before you came in; he was asking if I wanted any help."

"We've got forty men from outside the division now."

"Not manpower, Arthur."

"I see." Milton knew what Davies was talking about. This was not a case of murder, but the top brass would be arguing the toss about morale, public image, and the importance of an early arrest. "They want to bring in the glamour boys?"

"An offer, Arthur, just an offer."

"Toms was our man, sir."

Davies grinned mirthlessly. "Keep it in the family, eh! Look after our own, and all that rubbish? I don't like vendettas."

"I didn't...."

"I know, I know, but I want this bastard in one piece."

"Yes, sir."

"And so does Mr Miller."

"Yes, sir."

20

"It'll be a flog," Davies mused. "There's something funny about this one. A lot of it will fall on you."

"Yes, sir."

"I thanked Mr Miller, and told him that we had everything in hand."

"We have."

"We better have. It wouldn't be much of a mark to fall down on this one."

"No."

"I don't mean personally : I've overstayed my welcome as it is; I'll not be promoted now. I don't mean it that way at all, but I've done nearly thirty years, and if I haven't learned enough in that time to take some layabout who blinds an unarmed copper I've been wasting my time, haven't I?"

"I see what you mean."

Davies laughed. "Well, don't look so bloody miserable about it. You look like a bloody owl."

"I'm thinking about Toms."

"So am I. But remember this, Arthur, it's a case—first and last, a case—it's not a bloody crusade."

"I know."

"Good. Toms should be able to talk in a day or so; he might be able to tell us something. If not it's going to be a lot of leg-work. I'll have a word with the ballistics man tomorrow, and he might give us something, though I doubt it. It must have been a shotgun."

"It doesn't make sense, though."

"What doesn't?"

"That it was a shotgun. I've seen a few; there was that one last year on the lighterman. At close range they tear you apart."

"I'm with you, Arthur; Toms was on top of him."

"It doesn't make sense."

"Toms might have got hold of the gun."

"Then the main charge would have gone past him. Newcombe didn't see any sign of it on the houses, nor did Lloyd, I asked him."

"Well, he'd know if it hit his house . . . but look, Arthur, that's waste-land, it could have gone to the side, landed anywhere."

"I don't see how; the car was up the pavement. Toms was shot through the passenger door, and for the shot to miss him the gun must have been poked up in the sky or pushed out of the car over the bonnet, and neither makes sense."

Davies communed with his pipe. "I think you've got something, Arthur. I can't see it gets us anywhere, but it's worth bearing in mind."

5

DAVIES was shown into a big vaulted room. The firearms expert, Mr Glenton, had a very keen eye. He was a smooth-chinned, trim-moustached man in his fifties. Davies had never met him before.

The room was painted in the usual drab olive green. They sat on the slatted chairs, and had a fine view of the sooty parapets of Whitehall.

"I realize, Mr Glenton," Davies began, "that as we have not got a bullet or a gun or anything tangible to show you I cannot ask you for a ballistics report in the usual way. What I would like to ask you is whether you can give me some sort of idea of what you think might have happened."

"Um, I see. I take it that you do not shoot, Superintendent?"

"Not since the War."

"I mean for duck—wildfowling, that sort of thing."

"No."

"Wonderful sport, nothing like it. Do you mind if I smoke this, by the way?" He waved a huge-bowled briar generally in Davies's direction, and started to stuff it with tobacco without waiting for a reply. "I've read the report of Constable Toms's injuries. The tattooing would be consistent with un-burnt particles of powder driven into the skin by great force. It would appear to be particularly noticeable about the face and neck. His face was terribly scorched. The amount of powder burning would indicate a shotgun cartridge."

"I have a witness to the man carrying a long-barrelled gun. It sounds like a shotgun."

"Very likely, but if your constable was near enough to be marked as heavily as he was by the powder the full charge would certainly have killed him. Was any shot found?"

"There was none on any of the walls of the houses, and the doctors found none in Toms."

"Perhaps you are not aware of this, but when a shotgun is fired the shot doesn't spread out immediately. For the first five or six feet after it leaves the barrel it travels as a solid column of lead. If such a charge had been fired point-blank at Constable Toms he'd have been shot to death, there's no doubt about that. It would have smashed into him with the force of a cannon-ball. There would also have been very heavy tattooing from powder burns, of course, although I'd not have expected it to have been quite so severe as this, unless the barrel had been greatly shortened. Tattooing is caused by the unburnt particles of powder that are expelled from the gun, and it's greater where the barrel has been shortened."

"So the tattooing in this case is greater than you would expect from a shot at this distance."

"In my experience, yes."

"According to the doctors all the damage to Toms was done by powder burns."

Glenton winced. "At short range that can be damn near as murderous. The gases generated by the charge of a shotgun cartridge reach several hundred degrees Centigrade. It was that heat which blinded your constable; it would be as powerful as, say, a dozen blowlamps. Whoever used that gun must have removed all the shot from the cartridge."

"Would they have known what would happen?"

"I can't say. At anything other than point-blank range—say eight yards—nothing would have happened, except a cloud of smoke. One thing I can't understand is that after a cartridge is filled with powder a felt pad is put on top to hold the powder in position while the shot is loaded. Now, if the shot had been removed it is logical to think that the pad would have been left where it was, otherwise the powder would have shaken loose, fouled the breach, and either caused a blowback or at the very least exploded nothing more than the percussion cap, and resulted in something like a damp squib. On the other hand, if the pad had remained it would have been impelled from the gun by the full force of the charge—it would, in fact, have become a bullet, and at the range we are considering would almost certainly have killed Mr Toms."

"A piece of felt would do that?"

"Anything would do it. It is the velocity of the missile that is the deciding factor, not the malleability of the missile itself. There is quite a simple demonstration of this in the old circus trick where you put a charge of black powder into an old muzzle-loader, and use it to fire a candle through a plank door."

"Well, if that is so what do you think happened?"

"It's very puzzling. One thing that could have been done would have been the dripping of a drop or two of candle-grease across the powder, allowing it to settle in the form of a thin skin. That would hold the powder in place, and would completely disintegrate when the powder was fired, but it is a very curious thing to do; I can't think what the point was. Was he just intending to frighten someone?"

"This trick with the candle-grease—would many people know about it?"

"It's not hard to think out. Practically anybody who uses a shotgun in the normal run of things would know about it— wildfowlers, gamekeepers, farmers, anyone like that."

"Have you ever heard of a man being blinded with a shotgun in this way?"

"Not at this range. There have been a number of cases of blinding by stray shot. At extreme range—that is, about 125 yards on average load—a pellet would easily enter the eye and cause blindness. The eyeball has the same consistency as a hard-boiled egg, you know."

"I'm obliged to you, Mr Glenton."

"I shall be very interested to hear what he was up to, when you catch him."

"I'll let you know."

Davies did not bother to shake hands. He was in a hurry to get into some fresh air.

6

DAVIES got out of his car inside the hospital gates. The intense cold of the preceding week had gone, but the wind was still northerly and a cold rain was falling. He walked slowly towards the main entrance, letting the rain soak into the shoulders of his raincoat. He came into the foyer and walked along the vaulted Victorian corridors, trying to postpone the moment a few seconds longer. Despite his long association with violence, Davies had never wholly lost the unease he felt when walking through hospitals; the sense of inadequacy before the authority of doctors.

Milton was waiting for him outside Toms's room, sitting on a bench set in an arch-shaped recess at the end of the corridor. Milton was beginning to show the effects of his lack of sleep, and Davies noticed, with a small shock of surprise, the patches of white hairs which showed at either side of his temples. It disturbed him to think that Milton, whom he had for so long regarded as a young sergeant, was now a middle-aged man. Milton got up.

"Has he said anything yet?" asked Davies.

"Not to me. He's still conscious, but the doctor says he is not to speak more than is essential. A nurse is sitting in there with him, and there's his wife and daughter."

"Still there, are they? Has he said anything to them?"

"Not as far as I know."

"If it's that crowded you'd better stay out here, Arthur."

Davies opened the door to Toms's room, and over his shoulder Milton caught a glimpse of the white blob of ban-

dages at the far end of the bed, and the faces of the three
women grouped round it. Davies closed the door behind him;
the three women had all turned away from the bed. The
nurse was quite young, but the two women sitting at the bedside had the patient look of women who were used to waiting.
They were very similar in appearance and dress, even to the
style of their close-fitting, helmet-like hats. A small bunch of
grapes had been placed awkwardly on the top of the bedside
locker. He came farther into the room, searching both plump,
grave faces for a sign as to which belonged to Toms's wife. He
decided it was the less plump of the two, who sat the closest
to the head of the bed, with purpling shadows under her eyes.

"I'm very sorry to disturb you," said Davies.

"The doctor has instructed that he must be kept very quiet,"
said the nurse.

"Just a few questions." He kept looking at Toms's wife, who
seemed to be examining him with disturbing intentness. She
eventually turned and said quietly to her husband, "It's Mr
Davies."

"Hello, old man. No, don't move," he added, as Toms
stirred. "I mustn't be long; you need all the rest you can get.
All I want is your story of what happened. Can you hear me
all right?"

"Yes." Toms's voice was thick.

"Take your time; tell me in your own words."

"I hardly saw him," came the whisper. "I thought it was
a drunk. It came by me, a white Zodiac, hit the kerb at the
corner, and the engine stopped."

Davies found himself nodding encouragement.

"I walked up to the car; there was only one man, very
young. I looked at the number as I went up to the car. As I
got near he opened the window, the nearside. I got up to the
car, and then he shot me."

"Did he say anything?"

"No."

"Did you?"

"No."

"Did he threaten you with the gun?"

27

"I didn't know it was a gun, I thought it was a stick. He didn't wave it about, he just pointed it at me."

"What did he look like?"

"Young, nineteen, twenty, something like that—he had a thin, refined sort of face, good-looking, fine-drawn. Large eyes."

"What colour?"

"I don't know."

"What about his hair?"

"It was fair. When he went by me at first I thought it was white. But it was very fair; I could see it when he leant out of the car, right under the lamp. Like it is on some girls, very fair."

"It wasn't white?"

"No."

"You're sure?"

"I've been thinking about it a lot."

"Yes, of course."

There was a pause, and Davies was very conscious of the rapid breathing of Toms's wife.

"Have you any idea at all why he should have shot you?"

The answer was barely audible. "No."

Davies picked his hat up from the bed. "I'm going now, old man. Be sensible, and do what you're told. I'll be back when you're feeling stronger."

He shook hands with the two women, and escaped into the corridor; he was surprised to find the palms of his hands greasy with sweat. He took a long time lighting his pipe.

"Anything?" Milton asked eventually.

Davies shook his head. "No more than we know already. It was a young man with very fair hair, so fair that it looks white under a sodium lamp. The light on that bridge is a sodium lamp."

Milton raised his eyebrows very sharply. "So he's not an albino."

Davies started to walk slowly along the corridor. "I never thought he was, and I doubt if he's known either. Toms had never seen him before, and it's a fair bet that he had never seen Toms."

"A nut-case?"

"Perhaps, but he'll still have had a reason, a sort of reason. He wouldn't have shot him for no reason at all. He was carrying a gun for something."

They had reached the end of the corridor, and began moving down the small flight of steps into the entrance hall. Two very young nurses came up the stairs, and Milton moved aside for them. He followed Davies's square back down the stairs, and moved past him in the entrance hall to push open the heavy swing doors which led out on to the asphalted quadrangle. Both men looked silently out at the asphalt—a shiny black now in the rain, like the carapace of a giant beetle. As Davies was about to go through the doors Milton said, almost to himself, "The gun's the clue."

"Why?"

"It's not usual."

"They're easy enough to get hold of."

"But not to carry about; a tearaway would saw the barrel off. And Glenton said the charge was unusual."

"So?"

"I think he's had it a long time. You're not that casual with a gun unless you've used it before—for shooting duck, or something."

"Refined."

"Eh?"

"Toms said he had a refined face, a pretty boy with hair like a girl, very refined. You reckon he's landed gentry as well?"

"It's possible."

"Anything's possible." Davies pushed savagely through the swing doors, and Milton followed him out on to the quadrangle. They walked through the rain in silence until they came to the car. They got in, and the driver swung the car away through the hospital gates. Davies lounged back in his seat next to the driver, his pipe hanging loosely from his eye-tooth, now and then belching great clouds of smoke which drifted back irritatingly into Milton's face. Davies continued to say nothing as they hissed on through the drenched streets; past the terraced houses of the owner-occupiers, and the big Victorian houses with their broken stone steps leading up to the battered front doors of multi-tenancies—of flatlets and bedsitters for Indian students and Irish typists, for Polish engineers, Jamaican bus-drivers, Greek waiters, Italian cooks, and the assorted lay-abouts of all nations. Actresses who were not acting, writers who were not writing, musicians without instruments, singers who did not sing, as well as plumbers who plumbed, joiners who joined, bookies who booked, and hookers who hooked.

They stopped at a junction with two filter lights, and in the long wait of listening to the hiss of the windscreen wipers, Davies took the pipe out of his mouth and said, without turning round :

"So you reckon a tearaway wouldn't carry a gun like that?"

"Is it likely? You can't hide it, and tearaways don't drive round on their own on a job—they go double-handed, if not more. They wouldn't go round with a gun on spec."

The car moved off again, jolting Milton back in his seat, and it was another mile before Davies removed his pipe again.

"I give you all that, Arthur, but it still doesn't get us damn-all place. I never thought he was a professional. Knowing what he isn't makes it harder. Snouts aren't any good on this, nor turning over doss-houses. He's probably tucked up at home with respectable parents who'd give him the top brick off the chimney. When we do find him there'll be a list of vicars as long as your arm to tell us what a lovely lad he is. It's the old story."

"I just keep coming back to the shot being taken out of the cartridge."

"Well?"

"Whichever way you look at it, a villain, or a madman even, ready to shoot the first man who gets in the way—both of them intend it for keeps; but this joker takes the shot out—what does it mean? Did he know what it would do? Did he think it wouldn't do any harm? What the hell was the idea?"

"I know the questions, Arthur. What I want are a few answers. I want the whys answered. Why this pretty bastard was driving a stolen car duffed up by a pro, and drives it so badly he stalls the bloody thing up a kerb. Why he waits for poor old Toms to come up to see what's wrong, blasts his eyes out with some trick cartridge, and then strolls off like he was on his way to a tea-party."

Milton did not reply; his mind was racing, but he could not find the right words to give his thoughts expression. He agreed with practically everything that Davies had said; the man who blinded Toms was not likely to be a professional criminal. The thing that had obtruded in his mind ever since he had first heard it from Lloyd was that of the gunman strolling away, completely unconcerned. It had acted as a magnet to all his thoughts ever since. Milton couldn't conceive anyone he had ever met doing that.

They drove another mile or so through the drenched streets before Davies again removed his pipe. "I'm going back to the station so we may as well drop you off at the dog-track; they've got a meeting on."

"Sir?"

"Show your face round the bookies; they've got their ears to the ground, and it all helps. I'll see you later on."

"Yes, sir."

The driver pulled the car up in the restricted area of a bus stop and Milton got out, his shirt collar saturated almost before he closed the car door behind him. The car moved off at once, and Milton went to find a security officer to whom he could show his warrant card. He was aware of the principle of not allowing subordinates to relax in familiar surroundings, to set them tasks within a prescribed framework, but as he went down the dingy tunnel with water dripping from the brim of his hat he was in no mood to appreciate it.

7

ARTHUR MILTON got back to the station in the evening. Newcombe was at the duty desk, sourly watching a very young constable slowly type out an incident report.

"Hello, Henry."

"Mr Davies wants you," said Newcombe.

"What about?"

Newcombe shrugged, and Milton walked past the C.I.D. room and up the corridor to Davies's office. Inside Davies was sitting behind his desk, gently tilting himself, first one way, and then the other, in his swivel chair. He was wreathed in his usual spirals of tobacco smoke. In the client's chair was a silver-haired man whom Milton recognized. Davies waved his hand.

"Come in, Arthur; we were just talking about you. You know Sergeant Lefevre?"

"Fingerprints, isn't it?" said Milton. "I've seen the sergeant in court."

"I wanted you to hear this. Sergeant Lefevre has brought down his report on the car."

"Oh?"

"If you can call it that," said Lefevre. "Whoever duffed this car knew what he was doing. The whole thing has been washed out. There is nothing on the wheel, gear-stick, handles, and I mean nothing, not a smear. There's nothing down the back of the seats or floor, under the floor mats, not even a hair or fibre caught at the seat edges."

"Professional."

"Very professional. It takes patience to go over a car like that. This one has even had the inside of the boot cleaned and the radiator cap under the bonnet."

"That's helpful."

"Don't keep him in suspense," growled Davies.

"Except on the inside edge of the door, by the lock. It's not part of the car anyone would touch, normally, as it's the passenger door, and whoever cleaned it probably did it with that door shut. As far as I can tell, someone got out of that door, probably slipped, and put his hand round the edge of the door to steady himself. Just under the lock where the tongue comes out was a tiny spot of oil, and he put his fingers across it."

"You've got a print?"

"Not a full one, that's the trouble. It's a partial—very clear, what there is of it—but no sixteen points of similarity: it isn't positive, nothing that would stand up in court."

"Still. . . ."

"Identifying single prints is a chancy business, a partial is hardly possible. But this case being what it is. . . ."

"Yes?" said Milton.

"I think I've identified it. As I say, you can't put it up in court, but I'm certain that it's the second finger of a man called Harry Carter."

"He's an old friend of yours, isn't he, Arthur?"

"I know him," said Milton, sitting stockstill, trying to make sense of another piece of the puzzle which did not fit.

"I was telling the sergeant before you came in," said Davies, "that Carter doesn't fit in with any of this. He's not a pretty boy with white hair, and he's been out of trouble for a long time now—makes a lot of money legitimately."

"A couple of shops."

"I'm sure it's his print," said Lefevre, apologetically.

"It's a bit of a turn-up."

"We have to box clever here, Arthur. One partial print isn't evidence, and this joker knows his way around. You know him better than anyone else here—you've knocked him off, haven't you? Do you want first crack at him?"

"I'd like to think about it, sir."

"He's one of the clever ones, is he?" asked Lefevre.

"Clever enough."

"I've asked for his file; it should be here any minute. See if you can find out what he's been up to lately. Anything; otherwise we go for his shops. He lives above them, doesn't he?"

"He used to; knows a bit about cars too."

"Ask Newcombe, he might know something."

"All right."

Milton went out into the corridor, and then into the C.I.D. room. On his desk was a wad of the latest crime reports—he stacked them up into the pending tray. From the middle drawer of his desk he took out his foolscap notebook and looked up the page on Harry Carter. Milton was a methodical man and he kept a register of all the arrests that he had made. In the eighteen years since he had come in from the beat he had made quite a few, and he added to his notes as and when he heard something—not necessarily from informers but from anyone, however casually.

Milton had a good memory, but experience had taught him that when information was wanted in a hurry the memory concentrated too much on obvious details and excluded those sometimes important scraps of knowledge which circulated vaguely on the periphery of consciousness. He had a great respect for written records and noted in his ledger the criminal file index of all his old clients.

He carefully read his notes on Carter; the outline of convictions, sentences, time served, and dates of release. Carter had been out of prison for nine years. There were also his private notes to remind him that Carter had blossomed sufficiently in his greengrocery shop off the Walworth Road to take over the shop next door; that he owned the freehold of both; that his two daughters were now in their late teens or early twenties— the elder had married a small builder and now lived in Surrey; that Harry went to the Continent most years for his holidays; that none of the people he employed to serve in his shops had a criminal record. The last line of Milton's notes recorded his opinion that Carter appeared to have gone "straight", and no longer consorted with known criminals.

He sat back in his chair and thoughtfully examined the ceiling. Harry Carter had never been a mug; he had only been taken either through an informer or by sheer bad luck. In all he had five convictions, the earlier two before he was twenty, for driving away without the owner's consent; for the first he had been placed on probation, and on the second he had drawn three months' detention. There was a gap of three years, and then, a year after he had married, the van he was driving had skidded on a clump of wet leaves on the outskirts of Reading. The van had overturned, and Harry had broken his left leg. He had been picked up by the crew of a patrol car, and in the back of the van they had found oxy-acetylene equipment. The gas cylinders were full, and they never got out of Harry what they were going to be used for. It hardly mattered. The van was stolen, the number-plates and licence false. Milton had led the search into Carter's shop, and had found ten thousand export cigarettes that had been stolen two months before. Milton had got a word or two from his snouts, but Harry had named no-one, and had gone down for three years. He was lucky in his wife. While he was inside she ran the shop, brought up their family, and turned away the odd tout who thought she needed consoling. Sally Carter was a very attractive woman who could make good use of the vocabulary she had learnt from a costermonger father.

Five years after he came out he was taken again, as the getaway man at the wheel of a Jaguar during the smash-and-grab of a wholesale jewellers. The tip-off had come from a snout who had both his legs broken when run down by a car a week after Harry and the others went inside. Harry drew eight years because he had tried to drive the car through the police cordon and had injured a constable. He had not been taken again. Although twice since then Milton had searched his shops on information received, each time he had found nothing.

Milton knew that the blank meant one of two things—that Carter had turned it in and gone straight (which is not anything like as unusual as respectable people believe), or the only other possibility, that Carter had moved up in class, ran with no mob, accepted a proposition at long intervals as a specialist when it was already set up, and came in for a fee. There was no doubt he was pie-hot on cars, but specialists were usually petermen. He glanced again at the final few lines of his notes. Carter was not a playboy, drank little, and did not womanize. His vice was gambling. He played the greyhounds heavily on occasions, but he was not silly about it. He was not silly about anything.

Milton got up and opened the door of the C.I.D. room. Newcombe was still at the counter, watching the young constable tapping away at the duty-room typewriter.

"Got a moment, Henry?"

"Sure."

Milton sat down behind his desk again, and Newcombe propped himself up on the corner; Milton felt the top of his desk move.

"That fingerprint fellow, Lefevre, still up there?"

"Yes."

"Anything new?"

"Might be—he's found a partial."

"That's no bloody good. They never match them."

"Well, he reckons he has; usually they don't have the time."

"Who is it?"

"Harry Carter."

Newcombe got off the desk. He scowled ferociously through the door into the duty-room at the dogged constable.

"That doesn't make sense," he said eventually. "He's been out ten years."

"Nine years."

"You'd know—you brought him in."

"There's not been a whisper about him for years."

Newcombe shook his head slowly. "I've heard nothing. I thought he'd had enough. He doesn't circulate."

"The only thing that makes sense, Henry, is that Carter got hold of this car for someone else, duffed it up for a job, and then dumped it."

36

"You going to have him in?"

"Mr Davies wants to have a go at his shops."

"Um . . . jump in on his family. He's a bit old for that one."

"I reckon so. I'd sooner watch him—he's not a talker, never has been."

"He's getting on a bit, though, Arthur. He won't fancy doing bird now."

"True."

"I'm with you really, Arthur, but the old man's got a point; there's a lot on his back. Talk or not, Carter's the only thing that's turned up. And you might strike lucky; no pro would hold any brief for this joker."

"Maybe, but it's still bloody daft to go in there with nothing to back it up."

"Well, it's not up to you, is it?"

"He'll just tell us to get knotted—then what? All right, it shakes him a bit if he thinks we've marked him up on the car, but if he runs to form he'll have a solicitor round here like a dose of salts, and if we push it on to court any counsel would have us out the window."

"It wouldn't get that far," said Newcombe gloomily. "They wouldn't offer any evidence."

"Oh, great—after that we might as well go round with bells tied round our necks."

Newcombe reflectively chewed the end of his matchstick. "You reckon this bloke Lefevre?"

"He knows his job."

Davies appeared at the doorway of the C.I.D. room. He had his hat and overcoat on and was pulling on his gloves. He was not pleased to find Milton still at his desk.

"You done anything about a warrant?"

"Not yet, sir, I was wondering. . . ."

"Well, move yourself, or all the beaks will be off to their country seats. Let your wife know you'll be late."

"Sir?"

"We're going in at midnight; don't want to frighten his customers, do we?"

Newcombe intervened. "You'll want a car, sir?"

"Patrol car will do; we'll want someone in uniform. Fix it up."

"Yes, sir." Newcombe did not move.

"If you want me," said Davies, "I'll be in the Three Bells with Sergeant Lefevre." He stamped off.

"Ah, well," said Newcombe, "it's all part of life's rich tapestry."

8

DURING the drive to Harry Carter's shop Davies said nothing. He slumped in the back of the car, trilby hat jammed heavily on his square head, the collar of his black overcoat turned up to his ears. The inevitable pipe wreathed out its spirals of smoke. Milton looked gloomily out of the window; the rain had stopped, but the wind was still northerly, and the night was cold but clear. The sky was dazzling with its clusters of stars. Milton did not look at the stars.

Harry Carter's shops were off the Walworth Road. As they came out of the double roundabout at the Elephant and Castle the pavements were no longer deserted. Alone and in little groups, sullen-faced men stood outside the closed doors of the shops and pubs. Huddled up in the collars of their overcoats, in the harsh light of the street-lamps, they looked both pathetic and vicious. Silently, with a blank hatred, they watched the police car move past them. In the Walworth Road proper they passed a group of youths who were kicking a tin can along the pavement. Davies grunted, and the driver half turned his head in inquiry, but Davies jerked his own head impatiently and they drove on.

When they were almost at Camberwell Green the car pulled across the road and drew into the kerb. Carter's shops had been newly painted. The rolled-down fronts shone glossily in the light of the sodium street-lamps. For a moment no-one spoke.

"Is there a back way?" asked Davies.

"Sort of; there's a yard in line with all the others; he could go over the fences and end up in the alley over there."

"You take that, Spenser."

"Yes, sir."

"How do we get in?"

"There." Milton pointed out the inconspicuous street door set into the wall by the far shop shutter. "There's another staircase inside, but it only comes down into the first shop."

"Come on, then." Davies heaved himself out of the car. Milton emerged through his door, and the two patrolmen moved out on to the pavement. They grouped themselves at the door, and at a nod from Davies Milton put his thumb on the bell-push. Nothing happened. Milton held his thumb on the push for a long time; eventually a window opened above and they stepped back.

"Who the hell's there?" came a voice. The constable stepped back into the light of the street-lamp. "Cripes," came the voice again, "it's the law."

"Come on," shouted Milton, "open up." The window banged shut. Milton pushed hard on the bell, and Davies thumped his fist into the door until it shuddered. At long last they heard someone descending the stairs. They were very light steps. The door opened on a chain and a woman looked out. Milton recognized her at once; she had hardly altered. She must be his own age, but no grey hairs showed in the blue-black hair. The eyes were still as clear and steady, the face unlined.

"What the hell do you want?" she asked.

"I am Superintendent Davies. . . ."

"Maybe you are, but I still want to know what you want."

"It would be better if we came inside."

"Oh, no, it wouldn't."

"You know me, don't you, Sally?" Milton stepped forward, and took off his hat.

"I ought to, Detective Sergeant Milton, but no-one is coming in here. I invited you in once before, remember?"

"I remember, Sally."

"Well, I'm a big girl now, so show me a warrant or shove off."

Milton sighed. "And I thought we were going to do this

40

friendly." He unfolded the warrant and dangled it in front of Sally Carter's face. "Now be a good girl and let us in."

"Now, just a minute. . . ."

"Oh, no," said Davies, planting his size eleven squarely inside the door, "either you open this door or we break the chain."

"Who the hell do you think you're talking to?"

"To a citizen who should have nothing to hide. You're entitled to invite anyone in or not as you think fit, but you're subject to the same laws as anyone else. You've seen the warrant; it gives us the right to enter and search, and that is exactly what we're going to do. So stop playing about and take off this chain."

Sally Carter glared at Davies for a full minute, and then : "I can't with your bloody foot there, can I?"

Reluctantly Davies withdrew his foot to within an inch of the doorstep and allowed the door to move forward : they heard the chain being drawn. Milton pushed the door and it swung open. Sally Carter was flouncing up the stairs. He followed her, his eyes exactly level with the creases at the back of her knees. The head of the stairs opened out into the hall with several doors. The first was open and led into a lounge. It was a long room running for some fifty feet over most of the length above the two shops. At the centre of the room there still remained a remnant of the party wall which had once divided the lounge into two rooms. At the far end of the room a television set flickered its blue and white side-show without sound. The furniture was elegant, the wall-lights diffusing a pleasant glow. Warmth emerged discreetly from the air ducts set above the grey fitted carpet into which Milton's boot-soles sank as if it were a sponge. A teak room-divider supported various pieces of colourful glass and pottery. Various things were hanging on the walls, including some very striking abstract paintings which Milton noted, with mild surprise, to be originals. Interspersed among them were hanging Chianti bottles, a pair of castanets, and a sombrero. It was a room that Milton would not have minded coming home to himself, and it was a room that bore the stamp of its mistress, who was standing now in the very centre of a thick white Indian rug thrown at an angle to the far wall. Her arms folded across her comfortable bosom, she glared with bitter suspicion at the invaders.

The constable hovered at the door, at a loss to know whether to guard the head of the stairs or to follow the others into the room. Davies moved his thick bulk to within a foot of Sally Carter. He had not removed his old trilby. He looked about him with some distaste.

"Well," said Sally, "are you going to start by having the sideboard out or do you want the lavatory first?"

Davies ignored her; he continued to perambulate around the room, squinting at the pictures.

"Is your husband in?"

"No."

"Where is he?"

"Why?"

Milton stepped forward. "Come off it, Sally, we're only doing our job."

"What do you want him for?"

"We want a few words with him."

"Oh, no, not that crap again. A few words. I've got a right to know what this is all about. Harry's been out of trouble for years."

"Then he's got nothing to worry about."

"Huh."

"Something or nothing, we're bound to look. If he hasn't been up to anything, then nothing will happen to him. Looking up old friends is part of the routine, you know that."

"Routine! It sounds like it with him—Superintendent, is he? Very trivial, I'm sure, to bring him and the rest of you clodhoppers round here at this time of night."

"There's nothing trivial about it," growled Davies. He glared at Milton. "Constable!"

"Yes, sir?"

"There's a staircase at the other end of the corridor. Go out to the yard, search it, and the garage. Once you're satisfied no-one's there tell the other constable to come up here."

42

"Yes, sir."

"Is anyone else in, besides you?"

"My daughter's in bed. You're not—"

"Get her up."

"I'm going to ring my solicitor."

"Ring who you like once you've got your daughter up. Start searching this room, sergeant."

"Who the hell do you think you are?"

"What's in here, Sally?"

"Look what you're doing, that's my china."

"Mum!" A very pretty girl in her teens was standing in the door. She wore a short nightdress; her hair, as dark as her mother's, was held back from her face by a ribbon. "Mum, what's the matter—someone's just gone down to the yard?"

"It's the police, darling, don't be frightened. I'll come back with you." She took her daughter out.

"I want this room gone over, Milton."

"Yes, sir."

"And I mean gone over."

"I know what you mean, sir."

"You soft on her or something?"

"She's not bent, never has been."

"What's she doing with Carter, then, walking in her sleep?"

"He's lucky in his wife, that's all."

Davies glared at the second constable, who had appeared at the door of the lounge.

"I was told to report up here, sir."

"Yes, that's right, follow me." He turned at the door. "And I mean a really thorough job."

Milton turned back to the open sideboard and methodically began to examine each piece of crockery, then he looked at the back of the sideboard, the under-side of the drawers, and patiently examined each piece of the fantastic miscellany they contained—recipes torn from magazines, old letters, half-finished knitting, boxes of pins, paper-clips, pieces of string, rusted door-keys, foreign stamps. It was all very ordinary, so much like the rubbish that collected in his own sideboard that he began to feel at home.

He finished at the sideboard and moved across to the easy-chairs, removed the cushions, felt down the backs of the seats, even turned the chairs upside down, but there was no hessian tacking; the upholstery had been properly insewn, and had not been tampered with. He moved across the room and began to examine the pottery collection.

Across the hall, in the main bedroom, Davies discovered that sweat was trickling down the bridge of his nose. He still wore his heavy overcoat, which was as thick as a horse blanket, and each time he bent to examine the bottom of one of Harry Carter's built-in wardrobes heat from the warming ducts struck him full in the face with an insidious force. It did not improve his temper.

Constable Spenser was cautiously examining the contents of the dressing-table; he was very methodical, carefully putting to one side of the mirror the paraphernalia he had already scrutinized. As Davies straightened up to wipe his forehead he found Spenser solemnly examining the inside of a lipstick container, and for no logical reason it irritated him greatly.

"What the hell do you expect to find in there, Spenser?"

"Sir?"

"What do you think we're looking for?"

"As you said, sir, anything suspicious."

Davies snorted and went past him into the hall. For a moment he stood in the doorway of the lounge and watched Milton complete his neat and careful examination of a Spanish wineskin which was hanging on the wall above the fireplace. It hung next to a meerschaum pipe and a pair of castanets.

"Well?"

"I've been over it all. The carpet is fitted and tacked, there's nothing round the edges, nothing anywhere; a complete blank."

"Well, don't look so supercilious about it."

Milton held his gaze for a moment with a completely blank expression. Davies felt ridiculous. He wiped the sweat from his forehead, and took his time lighting up his pipe before he looked up again.

"We're not doing very well, are we, Arthur?"

44

"No?"

"Found nothing, and don't even know where Carter's gone; out on a job for all we know."

"I doubt that."

"Why would she make such a big secret of it, then?"

"She just feels stroppy; we've put him away twice before. He's been out nine years, and they're doing all right. She isn't going to help anyone end that."

"All right, Arthur, you're the expert on Carter—where would you look?"

"If he's still duffing cars he'd need the gear, and that would be in a lock-up. He wouldn't do them in his own garage. And if we did find the lock-up and it didn't have a car we'd be back where we started. All that the gear shows is that he's keen on cars; it doesn't prove he's a tea-leaf. What he'd have here are the keys and whatever he used to do the licences. It takes time, and he would need that to be handy. But not up here; somewhere down in that office of his, probably. His wife wouldn't know what he was doing. He wouldn't risk having to bring it in from somewhere else."

"I'll buy that, Arthur, since you've got such a high opinion of his wife."

"She'd have to have changed round completely, and people don't do that once they've grown up, do they?"

"No, but women with kids do anything for them, and that means looking out for the father."

"It's because of the kids that she wouldn't."

"All right, Arthur, go and see her; tell her what a bastard I am, soap her up a bit. See what you can get."

"O.K."

Milton knocked on the door of the bedroom and got no answer. He opened the door slightly, to be met by a sullen scowl from Sally Carter. She was sitting on the edge of the bed next to her daughter. Neither spoke to him. Milton produced his packet of cigarettes and, uninvited, sat down next to Sally Carter. He held the packet out to her, but she turned her nose up. He looked around the room. The paintwork was an immaculate pink, merging beautifully with the wallpaper of silver stripes and little pink roses. Above the little bed were pinned large coloured magazine pictures of the Beatles and some other entertainers whom Milton could not recognize. Among them were photographs of ponies, kittens, and dogs. By the side of the bed was a long-haired rug, dyed pink. It was very warm, and Milton felt a great desire to fall back against the pillows and drop into a world that was warm, pink, and without problems. When he looked back it was into the intense gaze of Sally Carter. Her eyes were slightly swollen, and he realized that she had been crying.

"Well, Sally?"

"Well, what?"

"This is all very sad."

"Is it?"

"Why can't you leave Dad alone?" said the girl fiercely.

"God, what it must be to be a policeman," said Sally Carter. "Don't you ever get sick of pushing people around in your lousy job?"

"It's a lousy job when you have to do lousy things. I wouldn't like anyone coming into my place either. I don't enjoy it."

"Why do it, then?"

"Someone has to do it, so it may as well be me. If it wasn't it might be someone who did enjoy it."

"Like your fat-gutted Superintendent—he enjoys it, all right."

"You're not tough, Sally, so stop pretending that you are. Mr Davies isn't a bully; he's in a bad mood, and you gave him some lip, that's all."

"You haven't found anything, is that it, so they've sent you in here to soft-soap me? I've got nothing for you, Mr Milton, so just go back and tell them, and leave me alone."

"I came to tell you why we were here, Sally, why we've got a search-warrant, and why we're looking for Harry. If you don't want to tell me where he is after I've explained, that's up to you. We'll find him, anyway; and if we have to go looking he'll be the only one to suffer. Harry's got a respectable name now and a good business. It's stupid to throw all that away, just out of cussedness. We want to talk to him, and if we have to chase him all over London to do it we will. If he's in the clear that's the end of it."

"Harry's straight. He'd cut his arm off rather than do anything to hurt his family again. Just because he was in trouble once, any time anything goes wrong. . . ."

"Sally, Sally, I haven't been here for years. I'm not the Gestapo; we don't get search-warrants without good reason." He glanced across her to the daughter, who was glaring at him with burning eyes. "Do you want to hear this on your own?"

"We've got no secrets in this family," spat the girl.

"All right, Jill." Sally suddenly looked much older. "What is it about?"

"You've read the papers," said Milton, "so you've read about Police Constable Toms, who. . . ."

"Oh, my Christ! Not that, not Harry."

"No," said Milton, "I don't think so either, but this is where it all leads to."

"Oh, God."

The girl jumped up, so violently that Milton thought that she was going to throw herself at him. "You're mad, bloody raving mad."

"Perhaps," said Milton quietly. The girl sat down again and put her arm round her mother.

"Harry wouldn't have anything to do with a thing like that." Sally began to cry.

"Where is he?"

"So that you can drag him off?"

"We want him to come with us, that's all. We'll all go down to the station and we'll talk to him. He's got something to tell us, and if he does tell us he'll be all right. It's different this time. If you don't see that, then I'm just wasting my time. A decent man, with a wife and family, got shot in the face. He was blinded—it was a miracle that he wasn't killed. Do you realize what that means, to him, to his wife? He's just about our age, Sally, and he'll never see his wife again, or his daughter, or any of his grandchildren when they come along. That's the reason why Mr Davies came in here looking as if he were ready to go through a brick wall."

There was an abrupt knock, and the bedroom door opened. Davies's head appeared, and both women looked at him, transfixed. Davies motioned with his head and Milton got up very carefully from the bed and walked to the door. Davies allowed him to pass, and then closed the door behind him.

"Did you get anything?"

"I'd just explained why we wanted him."

"Let her stew a minute, then—it might sink in." He led the way back into the lounge. Spenser stood by the far window, holding a dirty plastic bag: on the table was a huge mass of car keys, held on individual rings, looped through with string.

"Where were they?"

"In the garden, at the back of the garage, in a hole under the dustbin."

"They never learn, do they?" said Davies cheerfully. "There's no car out there. He's in it, I suppose. We'll have to get the number."

"I'll go and see his wife again."

"Show her these." Davies threw him the keys. "Ask her if she's emptied the dustbin lately."

When Milton got back to the bedroom both women were standing, the girl comforting her mother, who had been weeping copiously. They turned as he came in, and Sally Carter opened her mouth to speak when she saw the keys.

"What are they?"

"Car keys, Sally, out of your garden."

"They can't be."

"Under the dustbin."

"Our dustbin is on a paving-stone," said the girl.

"And under that is a hole."

Sally Carter sat down heavily on the bed. "The fool, the bloody fool! Why should he do it, Mr Milton—where's the sense?"

"None, Sally; there never is."

"It can't be true, he promised me. I would have known.

48

I've searched, I've looked, I would have known something."

"Not if he didn't want you to; you're not here all the time, any more than he is. Where did he go tonight?"

"The dogs."

"Where?"

"The White City."

Milton looked at his watch. "The last race was over three hours ago."

"He goes on to a club, a gambling club. It's his night out."

"Which club?"

"Anywhere, they're all over the place, aren't they? They make it so easy for them now."

"And you—didn't you ever wonder what he used for money?"

"He never took it from us; he uses five-bob chips."

"He wins," said the girl. "Sometimes a lot; he's won over a thousand pounds, hasn't he, Mum?"

Sally Carter smiled bitterly.

Milton sighed. "What's the number of his car, Sally?"

"Find out!" spat the daughter.

"It's a cream and maroon Cresta, ZXT 920C."

"Mum."

"Harry bought it out of his winnings."

"Mum."

"And we all went to Alicante in it. You can't miss it. It's got GB plates on the back. We all thought how marvellous he was, buying it out of his winnings, just like getting it for nothing."

"Mum!"

"Oh, God," said Sally Carter, "I really thought he'd stopped. We had everything. He swore I'd never have to worry about any of that again. What a bloody fool he's made of me!"

"It's not you who's the fool."

He went out.

Davies was looking very pleased with himself when Milton

descended the stairs into the back of the shop. He was sitting on a kitchen chair, crammed into a cubby hole set beneath the stairs. Most of the space was taken up by an old roll-top desk. Davies had the receiver of Harry Carter's telephone pressed to his ear. He looked up as Milton appeared, and replaced the receiver.

"Have any luck, Arthur?"

"He's up West, punting; that's where she thinks the money comes from."

"Oh, does she? We've found something else. See the markings on these orange crates? They're part of a lorry-load knocked off in Hornsey last week."

"Any log-books?"

"No." Davies rifled through the papers on top of the desk. "But the gear's all here, pens, ink-remover, outline stamp."

"No log-books, licences. . . ."

"You want jam on it. He'd be a right mug to leave them lying about."

"He won't be hard to pick up; he's in a Cresta, ZXT 920C, or I could wait for him; he'll be back."

"No, I want him brought in. Get on to Newcombe and arrange it."

"Any charge?"

"To assist us in our inquiries, but tell them not to take no for an answer; I want him brought in. If he insists they can bring him in on this lot." Davies juggled a Jaffa orange in his hand. "There ought to be something else in this lot, Arthur; have a look through them."

"Here?"

"No, take them with you. We're going back."

Davies lumbered off to ascend the stairs; when he was half-way up he stopped to raise his previously irremovable trilby.

"Come down, Mrs Carter; we're taking one or two things, and we have to give you a receipt."

Sally Carter came slowly down the stairs. She had thrown a coat round her shoulders. She looked numbed. Constable Spenser handed her his careful list of the orange crates. She looked at it dumbly : Milton, not wishing to meet her eye, busied himself in writing out a receipt for the contents of Carter's desk. She took it from him without a word, and at a nod from Davies he tipped his hat and made his way back up the stairs. Behind him Davies again removed his old trilby to bow Sally Carter up the stairs ahead of him. His nauseating politeness was a sure sign he was very pleased with himself.   .

9

HARRY CARTER was a short, muscular man with thinning black hair; his plump cheeks could have cast him as anyone's favourite uncle, but, propelled now into the C.I.D. room by Newcombe, he looked less than happy. Milton rose from behind his desk in honour of the call.

"Have a chair, Harry; I've been looking forward to seeing you."

"Have it yourself, Milton. I'm not staying."

"Don't be like that; it's clean, won't make a mark on that eighty-guinea suit you happen to be wearing."

"This is a dead liberty, Milton. I get knocked off in the street like some drunk; that big berk won't let me near a phone; I'm carted down here, not allowed to call my wife. You know my wife, Milton, she'll go bloody raving mad."

"Sit down, Harry, and have a cigarette."

"Stuff your cigarettes. I've been straight for ten years. I pay my rates and taxes. I pay your bloody wages, come to that."

"Give it a rest, Harry; I've got a few questions."

"Stuff your questions and stuff you. If there's a charge I want my solicitor here. If there isn't I'm walking out; which is it?"

"Shut up and sit down. I've told you, I've got something to say to you, Harry Boy, and you're going to listen if I have to get Newcombe in here to sit on you while I say it."

"Oh, big stuff. What sort of a green yob do you think I am?"

52

"We turned your drum over tonight, Harry, and just for a start we found enough car-keys under your dustbin to fill Wembley Stadium."

Carter sat down on the chair.

"And we found three gross of oranges with a mark on the crates that said they were knocked off in Hornsey last week. Your wife's dead worried about you, all right. The way she carried on tonight you'll be better off inside."

"Oh, Christ."

"We found the pens as well—funny sort of collection for a greengrocer; there was this bloody great bottle of ink-eradicator and this outline stamp which you must find dead handy when you're bagging up the spuds."

Carter breathed heavily and said nothing.

"A greedy little man, that's what you are, Harry. You've got a good business, good family, a great-looking daughter who thinks that the sun shines out of your left ear, a wife you're not fit to be a doormat for, a full belly, dressed up to the nines, and you still get sticky fingers. A load of rubbish, aren't you?"

"I don't know what you're talking about. A bloke comes up with a load of oranges, gives me the moody, shows me the papers, how do I know what's bent? . . ."

"Save your breath. I've got the invoice here, and the ink's hardly dry. I'm sending it up to the lab boys to see what they make of it, and we'll make a call tomorrow to the firm whose name you got printed on the top. As I was saying, Harry, you're just a heap of manure. Not that I care what you are, any more than I care about your keys or your bent oranges. Right now there's only one thing that I care about, and I care about it very much—a copper got shot in the face and blinded six nights ago."

Carter's knuckles balanced at the edge of the desk. "Toms—Toms—you're mad. The papers say—"

"Why do you think we turned your drum over?"

"How the hell do I know? Some grass—"

"No grass. We went there because of the car. The one that was ditched. We examined it carefully, very, very carefully; and you know what we found, don't you, Harry?"

Carter wiped his hands on his handkerchief.

"We've got your print, Harry Boy. It took some finding, but we got it. You were thorough, Harry, I'll say that for you, but not quite as thorough as us. We had a better reason for looking, didn't we?"

"For God's sake, I had nothing to do with Toms. I was miles away, I've got witnesses."

"Shut up. Do you think I'd have sent someone else to fetch you if I thought you'd shot Toms? I know you duffed that car, and I want to know who for."

"I'm not grassing."

"I'm not kidding you, Harry, I want that name."

"It was nothing to do with it. You know as well as I do that none of the boys did Toms. This was some kid, a nut-case. If I knew who it was I'd tell you; I'd have phoned it in, anyone would; it's not grassing to turn in a creep like that. I swear to God that car won't get you anywhere."

"I'll decide that."

"I'm still not grassing, whether I go down for a handful or not. I'm saying nothing."

"I'm going to have that name, and I don't care how I get it. It's up to you whether we do this the hard way or the easy way. I've got three names here: I wrote them down while I was waiting for you. I know what you've been doing, and why. You've been on the twist to get money for gambling. You lost more than you could take out of the shop. Sally would soon twig anything like that, wouldn't she? So you went on the game again. Now, you wouldn't fancy doing porridge at your age, you wouldn't go out driving, so you've been duffing cars, holding them in lock-ups, and getting cash on delivery. You probably didn't even knock them off yourself, because that could be a bit dicey, couldn't it? How much did you give the yobbos, a tenner?"

Carter said nothing, but he was unable to control the fidgeting of his fingers, and Milton noted that the sweat had begun to collect just below the hairline on his forehead.

54

"I've been through your file pretty carefully: you only deal with the big boys, don't you, Harry? It's all in here, and you wouldn't change at your age. The small boys couldn't afford you, anyway. If you really aren't going to say anything, what are we going to do?"

Carter watched Milton as if he were hypnotized, and Milton continued speaking very softly.

"The only thing we can do—knock over all three, and spread the word that Harry gave us the nod. None of them will be happy, will they? We'll find them, though, whichever one it is, and down they'll go. And do you know what we'll do with you, Harry Boy, we'll have to charge you with the oranges: maybe they'll wear your bent invoice; maybe we won't press it too hard. It won't make much difference, though, because there'll be enough doubt, and you wouldn't draw much—probably just a few stern words. You won't go inside, but the others will, and they'll start chewing it over like they do; there's not much else to do in stir, is there? They'll start thinking, there's Harry Boy on the outside, and. . . ."

"You lousy bastard."

"You weren't listening. I told you there's only one thing I care about. I don't care about you, Harry; the only use you are to me is to save time. Get in my way and they can chop you up outside the station for all I care. I wouldn't raise a finger."

"Milton, for Christ's sake, they'll do my family."

"You know them better than I do."

"Look, I'm not making a statement, I'm not repeating it outside this room. This is just between you and me. All right, it was more or less like you said. I've been punting, I got on a bad streak, you know what it's like, you have to play yourself out of it, you need capital."

"Don't tell me about your sad little life, Harry, just tell me who the car was for."

"So I had this car, didn't I? I did a good job on it, licence, everything, I washed it out, I went all over it. Where the hell did I leave that print?"

"The car, Harry, the car!"

"This kid came in, right in my shop; I nearly had heart-failure. In front of all my customers he came right out and asked me for the keys. Said he'd been sent to pick it up. I nearly stuck him one on."

"Stick to the point."

"I took him in the back and asked him who the hell he thought he was. He said they were in a hurry—a special job, and a lot of other old moody. He had all the right names, but he didn't have the money, so I phoned through and the boys nearly went spare; told me to hang on to him, but I wasn't having that; not on my own doorstep. Not that it made any difference, he was there while I phoned and he got the message. He scarpered, and then I found he had the keys. The boys went round to the lock-up but he'd had it away."

"How did he get the keys?"

"When I took him through I thought he was just stupid. I mean, I thought he had been sent, just didn't know how to go about it. It was only when he said he didn't have the fee that I put the call through. The keys were on my desk. He must have picked them up when he heard me getting through."

"What was his name?"

"I don't know, he never told me; just said he'd been sent."

"What did he look like?"

"Like it says in the papers: a kid, twenty, twenty-one, about my height, but skinny; a pretty boy with this hair like a girl."

"How did he know the car was in a lock-up?"

"I don't know, do I?"

"Oh, yes, you do. Who was it for?"

"I've told you all I know. I'm not putting anyone away. None of them know this kid, they never even saw him; they can't lead you to him."

"You're lying. They knew him all right, even if you didn't. That's why you didn't phone us: they told you to lay off, didn't they, to keep your mouth shut? They're a heavy mob, and you're frightened of them. I want the name, and I know it's one of the three I've got here. It's up to you."

"And what happens to me?"

"I don't know what's going to happen to you, Harry, but I'll tell you this: whatever happens to you will be a damn sight harder if I get nothing than if I do."

"Can't you keep me out of it, fix it up somehow?"

"We'll see."

"You've got to promise me, you can't let them have a go at my wife. It's not just me. . . ."

"You're wasting time. The name!"

Carter breathed the name.

"Griffen."

Milton leaned back in his chair, and for the first time became aware of the cramp in his back muscles. He slowly picked up the packet of cigarettes from his desk. As carefully as if he were choosing a vintage cigar, he selected one, and with due ceremony lit it and allowed the smoke to drift up into his eyes. Outwardly he was as stone, but every muscle in his abdomen was braced to control a shocked excitement. Griffen's name did not appear on his list. Griffen had not even crossed his mind. Griffen was big, the biggest villain Milton had met in the whole of his career.

"Give us a fag, for God's sake."

Milton pushed the packet towards Carter, and watched him light one with trembling fingers. He noticed, as Carter bent forward, that the carefully combed hair at the crown of his head had fallen to one side to reveal a patch of baldness. Even the villains were getting old. Milton suddenly felt very old himself. It was difficult to recall that he had begun his spell of duty in another day, thirteen hours ago, all of which he had spent showing a different face to different people, carefully calculating the weight of his words, the effect of the pauses. In some ways, he reflected, a detective is like nothing so much as an actor—good at the fanny, as they said in the underworld. Well, after eighteen years of trying he had finally fannied Harry Carter, greengrocer and villain. He felt no thrill of victory, he simply felt very old and very tired. Wearily he began to assemble in his mind the next bout of questions that he would need to ask. He knew that he must strike now while Carter was still off balance, but, tactics or not, he knew with every screaming nerve that he would himself have to escape for a few minutes, if not for good. Davies could have this one.

He got up, went to the door of the C.I.D. room, and looked out. The duty constable had disappeared. Newcombe was still there, his huge head visible over the counter, noisily drinking a cup of tea. He got up when he saw Milton.

"Did he cough?"

Milton nodded. "Go and scowl at him for a few minutes, Henry. I want to have a word with Mr Davies."

"There'll be no-one on the desk, Arthur."

"I'll be here, I'll speak to him on the phone."

"O.K."

Milton picked up the phone and asked for Davies's office. When he came on his voice sounded thick; he sounded tired.

"Well?"

"Sergeant Milton, sir. I've had a go at Carter."

"Any luck?"

"He won't make a statement, but he told me he duffed the car. The boy came round and said he'd been told to pick it up. Carter says his mob knew nothing about him."

"He's lying."

"Yes, he is."

"Whose mob?"

"Griffen's."

There was silence at the other end of the line. Then a curious noise which Milton recognized as Davies's pipe being blown through the wrong way.

"Could he be lying about Griffen?"

"I don't think so. He's too frightened."

"Who's with him now?"

"Newcombe."

"Well, Henry won't let him relax. Griffen, eh! I think you're right, Arthur, he wouldn't lie about Griffen—it would be asking for trouble. What made him cough?"

"I said we'd put the word round."

Davies laughed. "You're a hard bastard when you want to be, Arthur."

"I think he's ripe."

"I'll be down."

Milton put the phone down, put his arms on the counter, and placed the palms across his eyes. He felt himself fall into a half-somnolent state. The telephone rang, but he was far too far away in his velvety black tunnel to be concerned. He knew nothing more until Davies touched him on the shoulder.

"Get off home, Arthur, and have a sleep."

Davies opened the door of the C.I.D. room, and after a moment Newcombe came out. "You look a bit washed out, Arthur."

"I'm getting old."

"Aren't we all! He coughed, then, did he?"

"Didn't he tell you?"

"Didn't say a blind word to me, just moaned a bit about his family. I just looked at him a bit hard to keep him on the boil."

Milton smiled weakly. "One of your hard looks, Henry, is worth a hundred questions."

"What you need, Arthur, is a good night's kip; go home and see if your wife still recognizes you."

"I'm going, but I'll put you out of your misery, Henry. He says he never saw the kid before in his life. He did the car up for Griffen and the kid called round and said he'd been sent to collect it."

Newcombe whistled. "What did you use on him, thumb-screws?"

"Only my spare set." He gave a gigantic yawn. "I'm going before I have to use one of your cells!"

"Griffen, eh! That needs thinking about."

"That's right, Henry, you think about it."

Newcombe leaned on the inquiry desk and scowled furiously at the rubberized floor-tiles. "Griffen." He was mouthing it for a second time as Milton opened the door and stood braced, allowing the bitter night air to shock him sufficiently awake to drive home. Frost was sparkling on the pavements like icing sugar. The windscreen of his Anglia was shrouded in white, and Milton cleared a space in front of the steering-wheel with the edge of a matchbox. His engine was reluctant to fire, and he sent up his usual curses, consigning to the uttermost limit of hell whoever it was who designed cars without starting-handles.

At the fifth attempt the engine coughed into life, and Milton blew on his frozen hands before he reluctantly put the car into gear and moved off. He opened the window to its fullest extent as he reached the edge of the forecourt. The icy blast made his eyes water, but at least it kept his head clear. He moved out into the deserted street and on to the corner where the traffic lights meticulously drilled non-existent traffic. Shop-windows glared out on to the frost-bitten streets, and the only moving thing was a newspaper which rasped along the kerb, propelled by the cold easterly wind coming up from Grafton Street.

Milton tried to visualize patrolling these streets, up all the dark alleys and windswept corners. He remembered his own days as a beat constable, and when he had had his share of winter nights, but it was now more than eighteen years ago. He had been a young man with hot blood: Toms was about his own age, and night patrols in winter must have been purgatory for him. Milton tried to imagine the aimless, miserable walk along the mean street by the railway line ending in the searing blast of a shotgun, and when he shivered it had nothing to do with the cold.

10

CHRISTINE WREN touched up her lipstick as she looked into the bronze-tinted mirror above the shelf that ran round the whole of Gino's Coffee Bar. Christine had been in the coffee bar for more than an hour, and in that time she had been approached by the tallest of three youths in tight jackets who asked if she wanted to go to a party "out Ken way", and had been offered a cigarette by a sallow-faced man in a business suit who had a nervous tic to the left side of his mouth and the unpleasant habit of inserting the small finger of his right hand into the left nostril of his thin nose.

Quite a few girls went to Gino's, and Christine stood out slightly because she had more poise. A slim brunette of twenty-four, she moved well with the rhythm of a born dancer; she could have been a secretary, a saleswoman, a dressmaker, or a receptionist. The last thing anyone at Gino's would have guessed was that she was a policewoman.

This was partly the reason why she was such a good one. In the two years since she had been working in plain clothes she had traced twelve dealers in Purple Hearts and other drugs, given evidence that had closed four clubs, and arrested twelve men on charges of indecent exposure. She had also taken in eighty-three girls under eighteen who had landed in London from villages and towns all over England, propelled there by either ambition or boredom; by brutal fathers, drunken mothers, or because they had broken into the gas-meters. All sorts of girls from all sorts of places, and they had all ended up drinking canteen tea in the little room behind the reception desk. Forty-one of those girls had returned home. Christine could only shrug her shoulders over the others. Seventeen of them had got jobs and were living out their lives in bedsitters: the rest were scattered somewhere in West Eleven.

Three of these girls had mentioned Gino's as the place in which they had met a man who had offered them pep pills and talked of parties where they could meet influential people. He was about forty, very well-dressed, and apparently rich; he had a car, and talked of his house in Belgravia. He had told two of the girls that he owned a club, the third that he was a portrait-painter, and had sketched her on the inside of a cigarette packet. The description fitted that of a Harold Bilton, sometimes known as Geoffrey de Retz, otherwise the Creep. Christine Wren had studied the police photographs of Bilton, had read his file, knew his habits, his peculiarities, his method of operation, even the date of his birth, and the fact that his father still kept a grocery shop in Norwich. She would know Bilton at once. But tonight in Gino's, watching the failures and the layabouts—who were themselves furtively studying each other over their capuccinos—her mind was not fully on Bilton. She was thinking about Toms.

She had had little to do with him, and she knew that among the policemen of her generation Toms was dismissed as a nice steady bloke who was a failure, a constable after twenty-three years. It somehow made what had happened to him seem even more brutal. She had once gone with Toms when she was still in uniform to arrest a girl who had absconded from an approved school. The language of the girl's parents (only outdone by that of her nine-year-old brother) had been a continuous stream of obscenity, and Christine had been touched by Toms's concern that she should have been subjected to so much unpleasantness. It was an attitude a million light years away from the hipster world of coffee bars and discothèques. It was while she was thinking of Toms's wife (whom she had never met) that Christine noticed a girl who was standing aimlessly with her back to the coffee machine. She had not seen her come in. She was a small girl with long, fluffy hair, wearing a straight white dress under a black leather jacket. She seemed to be looking for someone. Her face was very white, and she wore thick make-up around her eyes which if anything made her look younger. Christine put her age at seventeen. Although the girl was very young Christine knew almost as soon as she saw her that she was no arrival from the provinces. She had a brittle assurance, and was able to shrug off the appraising glances of the layabouts. Her eyes moved steadily over everyone at the spindly-legged tables. Once she had surveyed the room a little of the aggression in her face softened into defeat. She turned back and spoke to the dapper Greek who stood aloofly behind the counter. He shook his head in a bored sort of way, and as she continued speaking picked up a cloth and became occupied with wiping down the counter.

Christine watched this little charade curiously.

The girl continued to speak to the Greek and he shook his head; he shook his head a number of times, and then he ignored her. The girl spat a word at him, and flounced off towards the toilet. The Greek followed her with eyes full of a weary contempt.

Christine gathered up her handbag and followed the girl. There was no-one else in the powder-room, which apart from the lavatory held two cane chairs, a small hand-basin, a broken piece of mirror, and a notice informing all ladies that the washing of stockings or any other items in the basin was absolutely forbidden. The lamp was about twenty-five watts, and shrouded the whole place in a dim furtiveness.

The little blonde girl was fluffing out her hair with a large metal dog-comb; she looked up as Christine came in. Christine stood next to her to comb her own hair, and was aware of the girl's eyes in the mirror putting her through a very close scrutiny. Christine looked back with blank hostility; she had discovered early in her career in plain clothes that to be friendly at the beginning only aroused suspicion. In this half-world an overture was regarded as either a gambit or a weakness.

She ignored the girl and opened up her handbag to replace her comb and take out her lipstick. She also took out a cigarette, and held it in her left hand as she applied the lipstick with her right. The blonde was fidgety; she opened her own hand-bag a number of times, and peered inside as if to make sure everything was there. Christine moved past her to the hand-basin and turned on the tap. It grated on the washer, but nothing came out.

"That never works," said the blonde.

Christine shrugged, took out her book of matches, and lit the cigarette.

"You been stood up?" asked the girl.

"He'll come."

"Yeah, so'll Christmas."

Christine blew a cloud of smoke at her own reflection in the mirror, and then looked very coolly at the girl while the smoke cleared. The girl's eyes wavered, and she went back to combing her hair, but she did it slowly as if she were reluctant to finish. Christine turned away from the mirror, carried her handbag over to one of the cane chairs, and began to turn over its contents. The girl went on combing her hair, but she altered her stance so that she was still able to watch Christine in the mirror's reflection. Christine took a long time searching her handbag. She took out a much-folded envelope, opened it, twisted up her lips in disgust, and screwed the envelope up savagely. She was aware that the girl had given up pretending to comb her hair and was now openly staring at her.

"You want a bomb, don't you?" said the girl. "You might as well admit it, you're dying for one."

"Who says so?"

"I know what it's like. Your bloke's scarpered, ain't he? Told you he'll see you here, and gone off with some other tart. That's it, ain't it?"

"What about it?"

"Look, I've got some stuff here. What are you on, blacks or purples? You registered?"

"No."

64

"All right, be cagey, it's no skin off mine. Have one, no strings. I'll give you one."

"Why should you?"

"You can do something for me. Let's have a drink of the lousy coffee they've got here and I'll tell you about it. If you don't want to, O.K., that's fair enough, ain't it?"

"All right," said Christine, "that's fair enough."

They went out again into the restaurant. The Greek looked sharply at them as they emerged. The little blonde looked at him as if he was dirt before she pointed to the coffee machine and held up two fingers. He pumped out two coffees without a word. The blonde paid, and Christine carried the cups back to her former table in the corner farthest from the door. After they had sat down the girl slid a tablet beneath Christine's saucer.

"O.K.," she said.

"What do I have to do for it?"

"You on the game?"

"No."

"You could make a fortune if you wanted to. This place is no good, though, nothing but creeps ever come in here. You could make a bomb. You've got the looks for it. They'd eat you up, but you have to use your loaf. It's no good dropping your drawers for layabouts."

"Oh?"

"You know Griffen?"

"I've heard of him."

"He's the bloke, knows all the nobs, the real ones—Lords and directors and M.P.s. The ones with real money, they're dead easy: it's funny, really, they have all sorts of creeps trying to get round them when they're up in their offices and clubs, but they're all like a lot of kids when you start turning them over. As long as you don't laugh in their face, that's the hardest bit: course, you'll pee yourself laughing when they've gone. They don't half reckon themselves. You've never seen anything like some of them when they've got no clothes on."

"I can imagine."

"There's one old sod, owns racehorses and yachts and things; he's got a skin like a grapefruit. You know, all grainy, like a lot of pimples, and it's cold and clammy all the time. Don't pull a face; they're not all as bad as that. None of them are dead lovely, though. Still, it's why they pay, ain't it?"

"I don't fancy any of it," said Christine. "Do you want your bomb back?"

"Don't be daft. I was only telling you not to waste your time round here. You're better off leaving it to the old slags. What I want you to do is find a bloke for me."

"What bloke?"

"My boy. Look, this is just between you and me, see? If you tell anyone else I'll have your eyes out. He'll be looking for me. He's ever so good-looking, slim, with lovely fair hair, nothing like these other slobs. He's a college boy, university and all that, dead clever. And he's young, young as us."

"That makes a change."

"You're not kidding—it does."

"Has he got a brother?"

"No such luck, darling."

"Well, if he wants to see you, why doesn't he? Doesn't he know where you live?"

"It's not that easy. I can't go back to my flat, and he's got to be careful looking for me in case someone sees him."

"Griffen?"

"Something like that."

"Does he work for Griffen?"

"He did in a way, but he threw him out. Tom says things, he's very quick—witty, you know. Makes people look ridiculous."

"Griffen wouldn't like that."

"His idea of a laugh is to see someone fall down the stairs. But it isn't only that, Tom took one of Griffen's cars so he's looking for him. Griffen mustn't find him: if he does. . . ."

"If he does, what?"

The blonde shuddered. "He's a bastard. If he brings me into it. . . ."

"Why should he bring you into it?"

66

The girl looked at her very steadily. "I told him where to find the car."

"I see."

"We were going to use the car to go off."

"I see."

"North, where he comes from. We're getting married."

"What happened?"

"I don't know what happened, he never turned up. I reckon he knows Griffen is looking for him, or was."

"Isn't he still?"

The girl sniggered. "I don't know. Griffen don't know where he's gone, but. . . ."

"Well?"

"I reckon he knows where he's been."

Christine sat stockstill for a long time. The blonde did not quite know what to make of her silence. She toyed nervously with her coffee-cup, and glanced once or twice towards the door as if mentally measuring the distance.

"It's not likely he's around here, is it?" said Christine eventually. "If he was going north he'd have gone already. I don't think he ever meant to come back for you. If he wanted to he would have found you by now. If he hears you're trying to find him he'll probably think it's a joke."

"He wouldn't do that to me."

"He's done it already. I don't think he cares if Griffen takes it out on you, either."

"You don't know him."

"I know enough, and so do you. You know what he's done."

"Do I?"

"He shot that policeman. It's the same description, the car, everything."

"So what?"

"So you should go to a police station and tell them everything you know about it."

"Get off."

"Now's a good time."

"Like hell I will."

"Oh, yes"—Christine closed her hand strongly round the girl's wrist. "I am a police officer."

The girl sat for a moment in stunned silence as disbelief flooded across her face. It ended in a shout of laughter that bordered on hysteria. It was so violent that she had to clutch the table to support herself: tears rushed down her face, cutting rivulets through her make-up.

She was still helpless with laughter when Christine took her out of the restaurant. The Greek watched them go with dead eyes.

The only trouble that the girl gave out in the street was to hang giggling to a lamp standard for about ten minutes while Christine tried to disentangle her. When she finally succeeded the girl threw her arms about her neck and blew in her ear. It was as if she was getting progressively drunk on some invisible liquor.

Christine finally managed to get her into a telephone box where she phoned for a car, and twenty minutes later she delivered the girl to the station.

The sight of Newcombe sent the girl into a fresh paroxysm of glee; she leaned on the counter and tried to poke him in the stomach, while Newcombe regarded her much as he would an unpleasant insect. Christine took her into the interview-room. Davies had finished with Carter, and he came down and tried to question the girl.

"Who is this Tom?"

"Tom—what Tom?"

"You know what he did?"

The girl was fascinated by Davies's pipe. She tried several times to remove it from his mouth. She smiled, she smiled at everybody; she was very playful.

"You knew he was carrying a gun?"

The girl smiled dreamily at the ceiling.

"There's plenty to hold you on—these for a start." Davies spilled the tablets out on to the table in front of him. "How many of these things are you on—twenty, thirty, a day?"

All the time Davies was talking to her the girl's smile became vaguer, her movements slower, but at the same time more exact, as if she was moving while submerged in water. She seemed to be falling asleep.

They moved her into the charge-room and booked her for unlawful possession of the dexamphetamine tablets. In her handbag, apart from the drugs, was a strange collection of items—two or three dress bills in the name of Gloria Lamarr, cosmetics, a man's gold wrist-watch, twenty-three pound notes, and some change, a packet of cigarettes, two very long hat-pins, and some cubes of sugar with fluff sticking to them. The only useful items were two or three photographs which Davies examined very hopefully. There was one of a middle-aged couple bending over a dog, another of an old house framed against the background of a small wood, and one of the girl dressed in less sophisticated clothes, leaning against the rail of a promenade. None of them showed a young man with fair hair.

The picture of the girl had been folded in half, and appeared to have been kept because of a list on the back of what appeared to be initials with ticks or query marks against them. The photograph itself was of the type taken by street photographers, and by holding it closely to the light, Davies was able to decipher the faded markings of a rubber stamp, "I.D.E.Photos-Porthcawl", and a number, "A 127843". He put through the message to the Porthcawl police, and then the girl was taken down to the cells.

Shortly before dawn the girl created a commotion in her cell. The night-duty policewoman was unable to control her, and Newcombe had to go down. Even he was shocked when he saw the girl. Her hair was no longer fluffed out from her head, it was plastered to the sides of her face by dried sweat. The make-up had gone except for remnants at the side of her nose and along the edge of her jawbone. Her eyes were inflamed and watering, her nose ran, and she shivered constantly. She was unable to keep still and twisted first this way, and then that, in an agony of indecision.

Every so often her body convulsed and she retched, sometimes without any result. Once, with a small moan, she arched back on the bed, her body as rigid as iron, her weight solely upon her heels and the back of her head. Then, as suddenly, she collapsed again on the bed.

It took almost another hour before Newcombe was able to get an ambulance to come for her, but eventually, at nearly five o'clock, she was taken, strapped to a stretcher, to the London Hospital.

11

WHEN Milton awoke he had difficulty in opening his eyes. His bedroom was freezing, and he shivered in anticipation of the coldness of the linoleum to his bare feet. He put his hand over his eyes, and found the warmth pleasant; pulling the bedclothes up over his head, he slipped back into a wonderful cocoon of warmth and darkness. He found himself thinking of Harry Carter's flat with its heated air ducts and thick carpets, and of the daughter's bedroom with its pink walls and long-haired rugs. Harry Carter would never need to put his plonkers out on a winter's morning on to cold linoleum. That is, if he ever felt like getting out of bed at all, sharing it as he did with Sally Carter. As Milton began to drift off into a hazy limbo he asked himself what the hell Harry Carter had ever done to deserve a wife who looked like Sally Carter.

He was still thinking of Sally Carter when he heard the telephone ring. His telephone was in the hall and he heard his wife open the kitchen door to answer it. He turned over in bed and buried his head into the pillow, hoping against hope that it would not be for him. He stayed there, drowned in warmth, until his wife moved the bedclothes away from his head.

"Your young constable is on the phone, Arthur—George Pawson. He says it's very important, like always."

"Did he say what it was?"

"Something about a boy; they've got someone who knows him."

"What!" Milton sat bolt upright.

"You get dressed, Arthur, it's bitter down in that hall. I don't want you down with flu. Remember last year?"

The cold air came across Milton's throat and made him cough violently.

"Put your slippers on, and something round your neck—it's freezing. He'll wait, he's in an office with central heating. And whatever's happened, I don't care what it is, you're not going out without a breakfast inside you."

Milton felt terrible. His eyes were gummy, and his throat harshly sore. He obeyed his wife to the extent of pulling on his trousers and sweater over his pyjamas.

He went down the stairs, and was further depressed to see through the opened kitchen door the washing-machine pulled out next to the sink. Milton knew what that meant; he shuddered in anticipation as he picked up the receiver.

"Yes, Pawson?"

"Sorry to hear you feel rough, Sergeant."

"I'm all right."

"I thought you'd want to know, Christine Wren brought a scrubber in last night, and it looks like she's our bloke's girl-friend."

"Where is she now?"

"She's in dock. She was all hopped up on drugs, and they're waiting for her to come out of it. Mr Davies saw her, but he didn't get anywhere."

"Where is Mr Davies now?"

"He's not here; home, I suppose. He said to tell you when you came in, but I thought you'd like to know anyway."

"Yes, thanks, Pawson."

"If you're ill, though. . . ."

"I'm all right. I'll be there in a couple of hours; anything else?"

"Only the usual stuff."

"Right." He put down the receiver, and caught a glimpse of himself in the hall mirror: red eyes, and his sparse hair standing up from the top of his head, blue chin. The hard light from the window was not at all kind to him. He shivered.

72

"You're going in, then?"

"I'm all right," said Milton. "A couple of aspirins will do me."

"It's ridiculous, a man of your age not looking after himself."

Milton tried to think of something to illustrate what he felt about Toms and how much worse it would be to be at home and out of it if they brought in the man who had blinded him. He could not think of anything to say. He had another fit of coughing half-way up the stairs.

It was over four hours before Milton reached the station. In a clean shirt, shaved, and fed, he felt much better, but there was a sour taste in his mouth, and he had continually sucked throat lozenges on the way up to get rid of it. They had not done much good.

In the C.I.D. room George Pawson was bent over the typewriter, fiercely concentrating on the laborious pecking out of a report on rifled gas-meters. He looked up with some relief when Milton came in.

"Mr Davies asked me to tell you to go up when you came in, Sarge."

"How long's he been here?"

"More than a couple of hours. He's a right iron-man, isn't he?"

"Yes," said Milton sourly. He hung up his coat and hat, and for form's sake looked over the wad of crime reports on his desk. After a minute or two he went out into the corridor and walked up to Davies's room, knocked, and waited for the shout.

Davies was lying back in his chair, swivelling himself gently from side to side. For once he had removed his jacket, and was sitting in his waistcoat, his shirt-sleeves rolled up above his hairy forearms. He grinned at Milton, and nodded towards the client's chair. He was in his element; some of the murk was beginning to clear, and patterns were beginning to form. Hanging from his eye-tooth was the foulest pipe in his armoury, the one with almost half of its bowl charred away. Stacked on his desk was a formidable pile of criminal files, turned face down to indicate that they had already been examined. There were dozens of them. Milton felt a twinge of admiration.

After Milton had sat down there was a moment or two of companionable silence while Davies sucked noisily on his pipe-stem.

"You haven't lost your touch, Arthur."

"Um?"

"You did a good job on him, a very good job."

"I knew him."

Davies looked down at the file he had open before him. "Have you ever had anything to do with Griffen?"

"I know about him."

"He'll be a bit before your time as a straight villain, though. He hasn't been taken for years."

"A right bastard by all accounts."

"He's that all right. I've been looking at his sheet, the one we know about." He picked up a sheet of paper from the file lying open in front of him and started to read aloud: "Howard Santos Griffen, born 4th July, 1909, Leicester Infirmary, mother Sarah Mary Griffen, factory hand; paternity order Arturos Santos, itinerant fairground worker. Taken into care by the County Authority, apprenticed as brickplacer to Corbett & Jones of Leicester, absconded, returned to County Authority as beyond control. First convicted 1927, obtaining money by trick, assault, three for assault, including assault on a prison officer—he got the cat for that. 1930-31, professional boxer, licence withdrawn by Board of Control. 1932, manslaughter while driving a motor-car under the influence of alcohol. Robbery, robbery with violence, assault, armed robbery, grievous bodily harm, assault with a deadly weapon— that was when he was with a race gang. Obstruction of a police officer, assault of a prison officer, two counts. Rape— five counts; using a weapon to resist arrest, attempted murder, theft, housebreaking, demanding money with menaces, illegal possession of a firearm, possession of drugs, carrying a concealed weapon...."

"What hasn't he done?"

Davies grinned, removed his terrible pipe, and squinted one leery eye along its stem. "He's never been done for riding a bicycle without lights."

"What about this girl Chris Wren brought in? Pawson tells me that she's a bit of a mess."

Davies nodded. "She's on these." He opened a drawer of his desk and took out a tube of tablets. "Lives on them."

"What about our feller?"

"It's beginning to come together. According to her his name's Tom, and he's a college boy. She could be lying, of course, so we won't turn the schools over just yet. Anyway, this is what it seems to add up to; he comes from out of London, probably gets an allowance from his family. He's up here to do some studying, but he just drifts about, takes drugs, and gets mixed up with the tea-leaves. Moves into Griffen's manor and starts living off this girl. . . ."

"A right load of rubbish."

"Not even a good crook."

"He lifted the car from Carter when the girl told him Griffen had the word out?"

"And he carried the shotgun in case they caught up with him."

"Instead of Toms. . . ."

"Yes—poor old Toms."

Davies carefully tamped down the burnt-out side of his pipe-bowl: it was making bubbling noises. "What do you think?"

"It adds up; it fits in with Carter."

"Yes, it means Carter was telling the truth, up to a point. It comes together."

"What about this girl; do you want me to see her?"

"No." Davies chuckled. "She's a right handful when she's happy. She'll be feeling a bit different about now, though. I'm leaving her for Christine Wren; first crack, anyway."

"She's a good kid."

"Very bright. If she can play it right we'll soon be on our way."

"We have to wait, then?"

"No, Arthur, we don't wait, I want a word with this joker."
He tapped the file on his desk.

"Griffen?"

"Be like old times. You know that bumboy of his in the Lagoon?"

"Topper Martin?"

"That's him. Set it up for me."

"Anywhere in particular?"

"I'm easy, but make it urgent."

"I'll tell him."

As Milton got up there was a knock on the door and a uniformed constable came in with a Telex message. Davies glanced through it and nodded to Milton.

"She's got a record."

"Drugs?"

"Thieving. All right, Arthur."

"Shall I phone in?"

"No, come back. If Christine Wren does get anything we'll need to move."

Milton went out and Davies propped his elbows on his desk, supported the bowl of his pipe in both hands, and studied the Telex message very carefully. It was to the point.

YR 128/12 PHOTO NAME IS ELIZABETH JANICE JENKINS DOB 10 JUNE 1949 NEED CARE AND PROTECTION 1964 SHOPLIFTING 1965 PROBATION 2ND CONV THEFT 1965 6MOS APP SCHOOL ABSCONDED WHEREABOUTS UNKNOWN ASSOCIATE GLYN DANIEL COLLINS CONV 1964 CARNAL KNOWLEDGE JENKINS 6 MOS IMPR NOW BLVD LONDON
INSKIP INSP

Davies picked up his telephone and asked for a call to Porthcawl. When it came through he exchanged the usual pleasantries with Inspector Inskip and asked if he could be put in touch with the officer who arrested Glyn Collins. He was in luck. Detective Sergeant Rogers was at that moment on duty in the Porthcawl C.I.D. room, and he came on the line with a soft Welsh voice that reminded Davies of his grandfather.

"I remember the case, sir, very unpleasant. She was only fifteen."

"Did he know?"

"Oh, yes, sir, used to wait outside the school for her. His wife made a scene about that in the court."

"He was married?"

"Yes, sir, three children."

"What did he look like?"

"Well, rather ordinary, stocky build."

"What was he—dark, fair, bald?"

"Dark, very dark, very thick hair he had."

"How old was he?"

"Thirty-one. He left his wife and children the same time as she absconded. They must have gone together."

"He's not with her now?"

"No, sir."

"Any sign of drugs?"

"No, sir, nothing like that at all. He hasn't any form at all apart from this. He's not a professional. He was always in work, never in any trouble until he got mixed up with this girl."

"What was his job?"

"Lathe-operator at the time, but he's done most factory jobs."

"And he has three children. Does he keep them, send his wife any money?"

"No, sir, I'm sure he doesn't."

"How does she live, then?"

"Public Assistance, I should think."

"Lovely people."

"Yes, sir. Shall I send you a copy of his photograph?"

"Do that. Thank you, Sergeant."

He replaced the receiver and sat looking at Griffen's file before he closed it and stacked it with all the others into the out-tray. From the middle drawer of his desk he took the thick folder of statements that had been collected on the shooting of Toms. He spread them across his blotting-pad, hardly glancing at more than a key sentence in each. He knew them almost by heart. He had read through them at least once each day since George Toms had been shot. Each time he looked for a detail, even a single word that had been overlooked or misconstrued. The man who defined genius as an infinite capacity for taking pains may not have been right about genius, but he gave no bad definition of good detective work.

Davies adjusted himself in his chair and rubbed the lids of his eyes. He blew through the stem of his pipe, showering the top of his desk with sparks and half-burnt ash. Once more he went over the same facts that he had been over so many times before. Toms had been shot by a man he had never previously met. He was shot because he was a policeman. The man who shot him carried a gun that was difficult to conceal, and he was carrying it at two o'clock in the morning in a stolen car. He almost certainly carried the gun because he was being hunted by Griffen.

So far as it went it made sense, once you allowed for the casual viciousness of anyone who used a gun so readily and deliberately allowed a man to approach as close as possible before he fired. What did not make sense was the removal of the shot from the cartridge. Milton had seized on that in the very beginning. If they ever found the answer it was going to be very interesting.

There was a quiet knock, and Christine Wren put her head round the door. Davies looked at her with pleasure.

"You're off to see this girl?"

"If she'll see me."

"We've found out a little more about her."

"Her name isn't Gloria Lamarr!"

Davies grinned and slid the Telex sheet across his desk. Christine read it very closely.

"Do you want me to show her this, sir?"

"It's up to you. It would be better if she came to you, but if you have to, throw it in off the cuff."

"I'll do my best."

"I've spoken to Porthcawl; whoever this fellow is, it isn't the man she came to London with."

"No?"

78

"No, she came to London with a man called Collins. He's in his thirties, and left his wife and three kids for her."

"I see."

"I don't have to tell you how much we're depending on this. As soon as you have anything ring through."

"I'll do everything I can."

"I'll be waiting."

12

CHRISTINE went to the hospital by bus. She toyed with the idea of buying fruit or chocolate, but in the end decided that it would seem too obvious.

When she saw the girl she hardly recognized her. She was sitting motionless on a wooden bench set against a wall. She wore a shapeless brown dress which gaped wide at the neck. She was clean, but there was something strangely bald about her; with her face washed, she had lost most of her eyebrows and lashes. Her face was very pale, and her eyes were sunken. When Christine sat down beside her she turned to look at her, but without interest.

"Would you like a cigarette?" Christine asked. The girl took it, and they smoked together for several minutes in silence.

"What will you do?" The girl did not answer. "What happened to the man you came to London with?"

The girl shrugged.

"We could contact your family for you."

"They won't want to know."

"Is there anyone else?"

"Not now." It came as a whisper.

"You're very young. You could start again somewhere else. It would be stupid to ruin your life over one man."

"It's my life. I live it my own way."

"There's a lot of difference between living your own life and committing suicide."

The girl said nothing.

"You're not stupid. You know what drugs do. You could be

cured if you wanted to be. If you go on as you are you'll either be dead or in an asylum before you're twenty-five. You're attractive, and you've lived off men. You've let men keep you. Do you think they would still want to once it starts to show on your face?"

"I might as well put my head in the gas oven, then."

"You could," said Christine. "There won't be anyone to stop you. It's not even a crime any more. But get it straight who it is that will make you do it. It won't be us, it'll be your friend Tom, and Griffen. Do you really like being used by men who treat you as a thing, who pass you on from one to another? Isn't that why you started to take drugs in the first place?"

"I should have stayed home, singing hymns"—but she said it without heat.

"What are you going to do?"

"What can I do?"

"Anything you want."

"Oh, yes," the girl grimaced, "he's done it on me, hasn't he? I should have known. I told him that Griffen would know it was me once he took that car. He's left me behind for Griffen."

"We can protect you."

"Like hell you can. Do you know what they did the last time they sorted a girl out? They used to laugh about it. They went into this pub where she was and sat looking at her for about an hour. She was scared to go out; she knew they would kick her all over the place if they caught her in the street, so she just sat there. Finally, when they got fed up, the chief one, Barney, got a bottle of brandy and poured it into a pint glass. Then they moved off as if they were leaving, and as they passed this girl Barney emptied the brandy over her head and one of the others dropped a match on her. It burnt half her face away."

"And they laughed about it?"

"They laughed about it all right."

"How did you get mixed up with people like this?"

"When I first came up to London with Glyn we lived in Fulham. He got a job there in a plastics factory."

"How long were you there?"

"Three months."

"What happened?"

"It was that bloody room. It was lousy, but he wouldn't move : he said he couldn't afford anything else."

"Rents are very high in London."

"We had a lot of rows." The words were coming in a rush now. "He got on my nerves; kept telling me to cook things, never wanted to go out. I used to be in that bloody room all day, and then he'd come back in and expect me to be there all evening as well, cooking for him on that crummy gas-ring or getting on the bed with him."

"He probably thought that that was why you had come away with him."

"He got a surprise, then, didn't he?"

"He left his wife for you."

"Yeah," she giggled, "that's all it was, really. I told him he'd got to choose between us. You know, she thumped me in the street and then went to court and tried to get them to put me away. Said I'd been leading her old man astray; some hopes. I couldn't get rid of him. He used to hang round my house, outside my school as well. He used to write notes to me, a right lot of filth as a rule. He used to send me bloody great valentine cards as well. I bet he never sent them to her. But it was because she had a go at me, that's all it was; I thought, 'Right, you stupid cow, I'll show you.' I just said to him one night, 'I'm off to London, and if you ever want to see me again you'll have to come now'."

"Where did you meet him?"

"In the pictures. He was on his own. He never took her out, even then. I was fifteen. You feel sorry for him, don't you? I can see it in your face. Think I did the dirty on him. He was a lousy bloke really, a right dead-leg. When she got up in that court and called me a tart I could have torn her eyes out. Talk about lead him on; I couldn't keep him off me after that first night. He was a dirty swine. He used to tell me if he'd been with her the previous night, or if he was going to after he left me. He was always trying to get me to do things to him

as well. I suppose his wife wouldn't. That's why he came away
with me; that's really why he left his wife and kids; and after
me I suppose he went back to them."

"No, he didn't. He lost them for good."

"Serves him right."

"Was that when you met Griffen?"

"Not right away. I met him through Barney Reid."

"And how did you meet him?"

"Through this caff I worked in. When I got fed up with
just sitting about in that cruddy room all day I started walking about. There's a street market off the Broadway, I used
to go there a lot and just walk about. I love markets and all
the people. This caff was at the top end, next to a betting-
shop. I used to go in there a lot, especially if it was raining.
Then this old Eytie who owned it asked me if I fancies working there, in the lunch hour. He was a funny old boy, but he
was all right, and he was all there. He reckoned that he got a
bigger trade if there was a girl behind the counter. The one
he had before had gone off somewhere. So I took it, didn't
I? I enjoyed it, that job. A lot of the street traders used to
come in for a cup of tea; they're a saucy lot, but all there, you
know, alive. Then there used to be a lot of the others, from
the betting-shop—layabouts, really. There was this big one,
Barney, who ran it—the others were all a bit careful of him.
I mean, they never contradicted him or tried anything on.
Well, he fancied me, said he'd take me up West. The others
had given me plenty of that as well, but I'd always laughed
it off. I used to finish at the caff by half-three and Glyn
never knew I worked there. If he had he would have reckoned
that I should have given him some of the money."

"You went out with Barney?"

"Yes, that's how it all started. He worked for Griffen."

"And Glyn?"

"He didn't like it, did he? He tried to knock me about, the
spiteful bastard, but I got Barney to see to him, and that was
that."

"That's when you began to work for Griffen?"

"Pretty soon. I didn't know that then. I thought I'd be with

Barney Reid; but after a week or so he told me to go up to Griffen's, and that was that."

"Did you like Griffen?"

"He's lousy like they all are, but when you're in it there's not much you can do about it, is there?"

The girl took another cigarette from the packet on Christine's lap.

"And this boy, Tom?"

"He was around. I'd seen him up at Griffen's gambling place sometimes, bringing people to the parties. Then one afternoon I went in a caff and he was there. It was after one of Griffen's parties. I had a hangover, but it wasn't just that. I felt. . . ."

"Depressed?"

"Like doing myself in. I felt like death. He came and talked to me. He said a lot of things; we talked most of the afternoon. I can't remember half of it, but it was all about what a lot of crap everybody told you, and the only way to carry on was to do the things you wanted to. It was what I needed, someone my own age. He was nice-looking, and he looked fresh, not old or fat and all saggy. He gave me some pills, and all of a sudden I felt marvellous. Then he took me out up Chelsea and we walked along the river; it was great."

"You saw a lot of him?"

"All the time."

"You were still working for Griffen?"

"Yes."

"Did he work?"

"He sold pills, sort of drifted about. He did all right."

"Did you know his name?"

"He never told me, not his last name. He was a funny bloke. I mean, I'd never met anyone like him. He wasn't like Glyn Collins or Barney, he was different."

"What do you mean?"

"He was clever, educated; I'd never met a boy like that before. You ought to see some of the books he read. He was always reading books; he used to read bits of them out to me. That bloke Sade."

"Do you mean de Sade, the Marquis de Sade?"

"That's right, that's how he said it. I didn't like it. Didn't understand it, really, it was all queer."

"Do you remember any other books?"

"There were tons of them, but I don't remember what they were. They weren't only in English. You see what I mean, he wasn't a layabout, he was educated."

"Did he take drugs?"

"Yes, but not many, just a pill now and then. He never touched the hard stuff, he sold it."

"Where did he get it from?"

"I don't know."

"Do you know where he came from?"

"North—least, that's what he said. He didn't speak like he came from the North. He said he was going to take me back up there with him. He came to London to go to college."

"Where?"

"I don't know. We passed it once, that's how I knew. We were going by it, and he told me that was where he used to study."

"Where was this?"

"I don't know."

"Was it a big place?"

"Bloody big—it took up all the street."

"Near Tottenham Court Road?"

"It might be."

"London University?"

"I don't know."

"Why was Griffen after him?"

The girl shrugged. "Money, I suppose. I think he held on to some of Griffen's money. I don't really know. I do know he got money from some of the people who went to Griffen's parties."

"Blackmail?"

The girl shrugged again. "He said we'd go back to where he lived; that's why he needed a car."

"Why the car Carter was holding?"

"He thought it was funny to go in one of Griffen's cars, but he needed a safe one as well. If he'd knocked one off just anywhere the law would have been looking for it, but Carter wouldn't report his stolen, would he?"

"I see; and you knew about this car, where it was."

"Barney Reid told me about Carter when I first knew him, how he always had one there, ready for Griffen. That's how they know it was me."

"What have you been doing since then?"

"Walking about. I couldn't go back. He was going to pick me up at the Victoria Bus Station, but he never came. I've been sleeping in a different room every night, hotels—you know, the Russell Square hotels, that sort of thing. I've been trying to find him. I thought, when I read about that copper, he'd have to hide away somewhere, but that he'd be looking for me."

"Did you know he had a gun?"

"No, but he had things hidden away all over the place. He was clever."

"What sort of things?"

"All sorts of things. He kept his drugs in a cemetery."

"What!"

"Straight up. He had to get some in a hurry one afternoon a couple of weeks ago. I went with him. It was ages on the Tube."

"Where was it?"

"Ealing, that's where we got off the Tube. I don't know the name of the cemetery."

"You know where it is?"

"I know the way. I've been back there. I thought I might see him."

"Do you know which grave?"

The girl did not answer immediately. "I'm rabbiting on like a good 'un, ain't I?"

"You can only be on one side or the other. Your choice has been made for you, hasn't it?"

The girl shrugged. "What the hell, anyway. He wouldn't let me go with him to the grave, he told me to stay on a bench, but, of course, I looked. I couldn't see exactly where, but

I saw whereabouts. He took some flowers, I'll say that for him."

"So, he went in with flowers and came back with drugs?"

"That's right."

"Was it a big cemetery?"

"Well, yes, I suppose so. It wasn't a churchyard or anything like that; it's not far from the Tube. You come out into the main road and go up by the cinema there. It doesn't take more than ten minutes. It's nice, really; as you go in there's lots of grass each side of the road, and great big flower-beds. It's all clean and peaceful : they've got benches there for you to sit down if you want to; you only see old people there, though."

"Is there a chapel for services?"

"I suppose so; the road goes right through a thing like an archway; there's a place on either side of it. Tom told me one was for the usual people and the other for the Catholics."

"Did you have to walk far?"

"No, the graves start the other side of the arch. There's five roads go off in all directions, then there's others going off of them."

"Which one did he go along?"

"The middle one."

"And after that?"

"You go up this path on the right. It's different from the road, it's not tar, just sand and stones."

"The grave is there?"

"That's when he told me to stay behind. On the corner, where you go off up this path, there's some trees and bushes. They've got them every so often, it sort of breaks it up. It's not just a marble orchard."

"A marble orchard?"

"That's Tom, he calls cemeteries marble orchards."

"I see; and after he went off you didn't stay where he told you?"

"Course not. I crept up and had a peep. I saw him bending over this grave."

"What was he doing?"

87

"Putting flowers on it."

"Did you see which grave it was?"

"Not exactly; it was about a third of the way along."

"Do you remember which row?"

"Yes, I remember that, it was the fourth row."

"And when he came back he had drugs with him?"

"I've told you." The girl looked sullenly at the floor. "And now you'll go up there and wait for him."

"I don't know; it's not up to me."

"What'll happen to me when I go to court—will you be there?"

"Yes, I'll be there. There's no need for you to worry; you've been a great help, and we'll remember that."

"I don't suppose I'll ever see him again. It's funny, one minute you're all making plans, ready to spend your life with someone, and then suddenly it's all over and he's gone."

"That wasn't your fault. He wasn't what you thought he was : you're well rid of him."

"I suppose so. He was clever, though; there can't be many about like him. That keeping his stuff in someone's grave—not many people would think of that. It's clever, isn't it?"

"Well," said Christine, "it's certainly something."

13

BONE COURT is at the back of the Tottenham Court Road. It is usually crowded with crates of empty bottles and dustbins. It also smells—a smell difficult to describe, but with the predominant odours of cats, fried onions, and rancid cooking-oil. The court was originally built to provide a rear entrance to the seedy office blocks and clothing sweatshops that were erected somewhere around the turn of the century. Griffen's place was in the basement under a café fronting Dean Street, but the entrance was in Bone Yard. On the door was a chipped enamelled plaque which said 'Lagoon Club Members Only'.

Milton pushed the door; immediately beyond it was a narrow flight of stairs which ended at another door. Milton let the outer door swing behind him, and was plunged into an almost Stygian gloom; the only illumination came from a bulb of something like fifteen watts stuck in a wall-bracket. Milton went quietly down the stairs to the other door. Inset in the second door was a bell-push. Milton put his weight against the door, but it did not budge : he gave a short blast on the bell. The door was opened by a man with enormous shoulder development and a built-in scowl.

"Card."

Milton opened his warrant card and the bruiser put out a hand which Milton avoided. "You can read it from there."

"What do you want?"

"To come in."

"Eff off."

"Don't be stupid."

The dapper face of Topper Martin came over the bruiser's shoulder. "What's up?"

"Bleeding copper."

"Who?" Topper leaned forward. "Hello, Mr Milton— social call?"

"It was."

"Course it is." He moved the bruiser to one side and held the door open for Milton to enter. The Lagoon Club was a long, narrow basement room. The walls were the exposed brick-work of the original storeroom. The floor was concrete, covered here and there by strips of coconut matting. The air was stale and warm, with great clouds of acrid cigarette smoke hanging over the occupied tables. There were about a dozen or so of these tables dotted about the room, some of them pushed together. The lighting was terrible, but Milton was able to pick out one or two of the faces which turned towards him before they were hurriedly turned away again. The bruiser went to join two men at a table towards the far end of the room; when he reached it he turned back to look at Milton, spat savagely on the floor, and then slammed himself down in a cane chair. On the end wall where Milton had entered was a bar with three high stools. Only one of them was occupied, by a girl in her early twenties with very long dark hair, who wore a suede coat and net stockings: she sat with her legs crossed, showing ninety per cent of her thighs. She had been talking to the barmaid, who had been leaning on the bar with her arms crossed. She heaved herself up as Topper and Milton came up to the bar. She was a tremendous woman, as tall as Milton, and built like a battleship. She was wearing a purple sweater, stretched to breaking-point, which had moulded itself to every wrinkle in her body.

"What d'you want?"

"Beer?"

"We don't sell beer."

"No, we don't," said Topper. "No place to keep it down here, but there's a couple of bottles of light ale somewhere."

"One'll do," said Milton.

The barmaid reached under the counter and came up with a bottle. She blew in a glass, and slopped out the beer. The froth rode three inches on the top when she slammed the glass down in front of Milton. Topper picked up a half-filled glass that was standing on the counter.

"Cheers," he said, and drained it.

Milton raised his own glass and took a mouthful without any pleasure; it was warm, acid, and full of gas. He put it down again quickly and brought some change out of his pocket. Topper shook his head.

"You can't buy it, Mr Milton, you're not a member. It's my pleasure."

"Nice of you, Topper."

"Pleasure, Mr Milton, always a pleasure to see you—in a social way, of course."

"Griffen coming in?"

"Griff?" Topper struck an exaggerated pose of surprise. "Griff comes in now and then, now and then."

"He checks up every day. You're a good front man, Topper, I'll say that for you, but don't take liberties."

The barmaid laughed and Topper shot her a look of intense hatred. The girl sat like a statue.

"I've got a message for him," said Milton.

"Well, if I see him I'll pass it on. If you trust me with it."

"I don't mind, but he's not at Barnes, or if he is he's too busy."

The barmaid sniggered again, and Topper turned on her. "Keep your face out, you fat cow."

"And you," said the barmaid.

"Keeps an eye on you, does she?"

"What do you want with Griffen?" snarled Topper.

"Mr Davies wants him."

"What for?"

"A chat."

"Oh, lovely—he'll wear that like an elephant's ear'ole."

"Anywhere will do," continued Milton, "when he can spare a few minutes. Mr Davies is very easy-going; he knows Griffen doesn't like stations."

"What's he want him for?"

"I told you."

"Like hell."

"Don't get ambitious, Topper."

"I don't have to take any old buck, you know."

Milton sighed. "Toms ever come down here, Topper?"

There was a strained silence. Milton could hear only the small noises coming from the tables as he stared with a steady intensity at a small trickle of sweat which rolled delicately down the side of Topper's nose.

"Toms," said Topper at last. "The copper who got shot? What do you mean, come here—what would he come here for?"

"You never know."

"I've never seen him in my life."

"And you don't know if Griffen's coming in."

"I told you."

The big barmaid spread herself across the bar to touch Topper's shoulder. He caught her eye and nodded, turning away from Milton with some relief.

"Give Mr Milton another drink," he said to the barmaid, and then, to the girl on the stool, "Ready, love?"

The girl slid from the stool and followed Topper down to the far end of the room. The men at the tables stopped talking, and a strained silence fell on the room, a brooding silence with an undercurrent of predatory excitement, as if some enormous animal was lying in wait for its prey.

Topper switched on an amplified tape recorder at the other end of the room, and also an ultra-violet light set in the ceiling, which suddenly made his second-hand dress shirt look as if it were fluorescent. From loudspeakers on the side walls came the tremendous blare of a record of *Mexico* played by massed bongo drums in the same rhythm as that of the human heart. Despite himself, Milton started swaying slightly in time to the music. Topper stayed at the other end of the room, leaning against the wall: he was careful not to look back towards Milton.

The girl began twisting to the music. She took off her jacket and flung it over the nearest chair. She turned and moved back sinuously until she was close to Topper, who put out his hand to pull the zipper at the back of her dress. The girl pulled aside the shoulder straps herself as she moved back to the centre of the room. She shook herself in time to the music, allowing the dress to slide down her body.

Milton felt a tap on his shoulder, and turned to find that the barmaid had moved along the bar until she was directly behind him. She was holding out another glass of warm light ale. As Milton reached forward to take the glass the barmaid inclined her own head until it was within an inch of Milton. Even so, he could not hear what she said.

"What?"

"Sh." She leaned forward even more confidentially. "That boy, he came here, Topper knew him."

"Now—"

"No." The woman moved sharply away and looked past Milton. He turned to follow her line of sight. No-one was looking at them; all eyes were fixed with hypnotic intensity on the girl, who was allowing one of the layabouts at the bruiser's table to unclip the back of her brassière. Milton turned back to the barmaid : she was watching him with an intent wariness.

"Griffen," she whispered, and drew a finger across her throat. Milton nodded wisely, raised his glass to his lips, and swallowed noisily. He put the glass back on the counter, and as the woman put out her hand to reach it Milton closed his own hand round her wrist.

"Ring me."

The woman's face went rigid, and Milton released her hand. He reached past it to the ashtray near her elbow, picked out an empty cigarette packet, and slid open the inner container : with the head of a dead match he scratched his home telephone number on the inside of the white pasteboard. The barmaid had retreated to the little sink at the other end of the bar, where she was very busily washing up glasses. Milton waited until he was sure she was watching him before he put the packet back in the ashtray. As he did so there came a mixture of throaty rumbles and snickers from behind him.

Milton turned to see that the girl was down to her shoes and a piece of sticking-plaster. She stood for a few seconds with her arms entwined above her head, and then Topper switched off both the ultra-violet light and the tape-recorder. In the comparative gloom that followed the girl could dimly be seen gathering up her clothes. No-one offered to help her.

Topper said something to the group at the bruiser's table, and there was a great hoot of raucous laughter. He came back to the bar, and Milton watched his eyes closely to see if they flickered across to the barmaid, but they did not.

"Well," said Topper, rubbing his hands together, "what about that for a bit of crumpet?"

"Bit young for me, Topper."

"Come off it. I tell you what, Mr Milton"—he leaned forward confidentially—"if you really fancy—"

"Goodbye, Topper." He buttoned his overcoat and went out without looking at the barmaid. As he came out of Bone Court it was drizzling with rain. He turned up his coat-collar and moved on into Old Compton Street. As he waited to cross the road he noticed a small man on the other side of the road standing outside a book-shop. There was something familiar about him. The man looked across and caught his eye just as a furniture van went by, but when the van had passed the man had gone.

Milton crossed the road and looked at the book-shop. A partition had been built close to the window, so that it was impossible to see inside the shop. On the street side were paper-backed books and magazines, most of them showing girls in black suspender belts in various poses on beds or bent over chairs. On some they were tied up or being hit by whips. As he looked at them Milton suddenly recalled that this book-shop was another part of Griffen's empire; and then it came to him who the little man was.

He went across into Cambridge Circus, and then, deep in thought, walked on up the Charing Cross Road.

14

WHEN Milton got back to the station Davies had been called to Headquarters to see Divisional Detective Chief Superintendent Miller. Pawson was out, but there was no note of his whereabouts. There was the usual wad of crime reports on Milton's desk, which he did not feel up to reading. He went out again into the reception area.

The duty constable at the desk told him that Newcombe was up in the canteen. Milton went up and found him. Newcombe was sitting on his own at the back of the canteen. His tunic was unbuttoned, and he was lying back, blowing smoke rings towards the canteen ceiling. He scowled a welcome as Milton bought himself a cup of tea and came over to his table.

"What have you been up to?"

"Turning over some rubbish. Mr Davies up at Headquarters?"

"That's right, telling them how it's going."

"That won't take long."

Newcombe grinned. "You haven't heard, eh?"

"Heard what?"

Newcombe took his time, had a last drag from his cigarette, and carefully ground it out in the tin ashtray. "There's a lead on your geezer. He's called Tom."

"Some lead."

"You're a sarcastic bastard."

"So my friends tell me; what's happened?"

95

"He's in with Griffen, all right, or he was; that's why he was carrying a gun, he had the boys after him."

"And this is a lead?"

"Do you want to know, or not?"

"Sorry, Henry."

"He's a drug-peddler, and Chris Wren got that slag to cough where he keeps them."

"Oh?"

"In a cemetery."

Milton was silent for a moment or two before he asked, "Where?"

"Ealing. Davies got on to the locals and sent Pawson over."

"What's his name?"

"She didn't know." Newcombe shrugged. "The other thing is he used to be a student at London University."

"It sounds like a lot of old mooley."

"It could be, it's only what this bird told Christine. It makes sense, though. He's one of those clever sods who thinks he knows it all; reads about it in books, de Sade, and all that other old cobblers."

"Above the law and all that?"

"He takes drugs as well."

"Who says?"

"The girl says."

"He's having her on; pushers don't take drugs."

"It's likely; a nut-case who thinks he's special—he'd likely take drugs. They'd make him different from ordinary people, wouldn't they?"

"She knows all this and still doesn't know his name?"

"That's right."

"And you believe it?"

Newcombe leaned back in his chair until it creaked ominously. He spent some time picking his teeth with the end of a matchstick. "I think I do—most of it, anyway. The name bit rings true; if you start bunking up with some bird, who the hell turns round and asks about names? You either know it or you don't. And if she was just telling a pack of lies, trying to get us at it, a dud name is the very thing she would give us."

Milton nodded.

"You been up to see Toms?"

"No." Milton was surprised.

"Why not—he's what this is all about, isn't he?"

"Well, I've been at it. . . ."

"Yeah, I know, and all you've been thinking about is this nancy boy."

"What are you getting at, Henry?"

"Nothing," said Newcombe, scowling ferociously at his canteen mug.

"Have you been up to see him?"

"Yes."

"Oh, hell—look, Henry, if you're passing the hat round. . . ."

"I'll remember." Newcombe lumbered to his feet.

"Hang on a minute, Henry, there's something I want to say to you."

"Tell me on the way down, then, I've had me ten minutes, and it's time I was back. I'm not C.I.D."

Milton let it pass, and followed Newcombe into the corridor. "I went up to see Topper Martin this afternoon. You know that dirty book-shop Griffen's got, on the corner of Old Compton Street?"

"Well?"

"I saw an old friend of yours outside there—Pinky Price. Looks like he's working for Griffen."

"Crap."

"Come off it, Henry—he was touting; scarpered, too, when he saw me—but I'd know that old prune anywhere. I'm only dropping you a word in case you're thinking of using him."

"Thanks."

At the reception area Newcombe turned to move behind the desk without a word. Milton opened the door of the C.I.D. room; as he entered the telephone on his desk commenced to ring. He picked it up, and grunted out his name.

Pawson's voice came through. "Sergeant, I'm down at Ealing, Mr Davies sent me—"

"I know all about that; any luck?"

"Yes, it was there, all sorts of stuff."

"Did you have any trouble?"

"It was a bit awkward. It could have been any one of a dozen or so, and it was a bit tricky. We couldn't leave any trace we'd been there, in case the relatives turned up. We had to go through eight like that before we hit it. He's a cunning bastard, they were in an airtight box, wrapped in plastic, and that was sealed off with insulating tape. They were in front of the headstone. The top of the grave is turfed over, and there are these slits where he hinges a piece back; it's dug out underneath, and this box fits exactly."

"What was there?"

"Pills and other stuff, all in little plastic containers. I've passed them over to the lab for identification."

"All of them?"

"Yes." There was a slight pause before Pawson continued, with a hesitant note in his voice. "I phoned Mr Davies and put him in the picture."

"Oh, did you!"

"I thought he ought to know—I mean, now we've taken the drugs out. If he goes back, that's it, isn't it? We'll never see him again."

"What did Mr Davies say?"

Pawson coughed. "He told me to report to you."

Milton grinned silently down at his blotting-pad. "All right, Pawson, I'm coming out. Wait at the station for me. Who's the divisional inspector?"

"Inspector Gray."

"Present Mr Davies's compliments to him and tell him I'm on my way. What did you do with the tin and the plastic sheeting?"

"Here, Sergeant, at the station. I thought they ought to be tested for fingerprints."

"Good, and get in touch with the cemetery superintendent. Ask him for everything he knows about this grave; he'll have a register or something."

"Yes, Sergeant."

98

Milton put the receiver down, stood up, and stretched himself luxuriously. He felt much better. He opened the door of the C.I.D. room and looked out. Newcombe was at the counter making a laborious entry into the incident book. On the client's side of the counter was a little old lady clutching a huge handbag.

As he waited for Newcombe to get rid of her Milton's telephone rang again and he returned to his desk to answer it; it was Davies. "Has Pawson been on to you?"

"Yes, sir, I'm going up there."

"Good. Now look, Arthur, I'm going to be tied up here until pretty late. You can get me here if it's anything special, but I want to talk to you tonight. I've heard from Griffen."

"That's quick—where?"

"At his flat, out in Barnes."

"Are you going?"

"Of course I'm going. It's tomorrow, and I want to know what's in this grave business before I do."

"Yes, sir; will you be coming back here?"

"Not unless I have to; I want a couple of hours at home tonight if I can. When you've finished up at Ealing call round. We'll have our talk there."

"Yes, sir."

Milton retrieved his hat and overcoat and went out again into the reception area. The little old lady had gone, and Newcombe was sitting down at his desk examining a duty roster. Milton leaned over the counter towards him. "I'm off up to Ealing, Henry. Pawson's been on; he's found a heap of stuff. Mr Davies'll be up at H.Q. for the rest of the day."

Newcombe grunted, without taking his eyes off the roster. Milton continued leaning on the counter, but Newcombe did not look up, and after an awkward silence Milton went out.

15

SERGEANT NEWCOMBE sat in the public bar of the Boxed Compass with his fifth pint of bitter in front of him. He had been there for two hours, and although he had put his raincoat on over his uniform it concealed very little. Newcombe knew that everyone in the bar knew that he was a policeman. He did not care; it gave him a sour pleasure.

There was a scrabble to his left, and the rheumy eyes of Pinky Price were looking at him across the little table. Pinky could have passed as a boy if there had been a sack over his head. He was the size of a fourteen-year-old, and his hands and feet were dainty, but his face was a mass of fine lines radiating out from the sides of his nose, mouth, and eyes, as if the edges of each aperture had been tightened to draw up all surplus skin.

Pinky was now sixty-eight years old; his days as a second-storey man with a cool head and perfect balance, of easing himself through fanlights and other incredibly small openings, were over. So were the palmy days of moving round the weekly markets with the cargoes of hijacked lorries. The young tearaways no longer bought him pints to listen to his stories; finesse was no longer in fashion. No-one was any longer interested in hearing how, in the spring of 1931, £15,000 was tackled out of four different houses in Eaton Square on four successive nights, so neatly that in two of the cases the police were unable to discover the point of entry. Newcombe knew that all the stories were true, and he often commiserated with Pinky over the recent fall in standards.

100

A very special arrangement had arisen between Pinky and Newcombe. Pinky was not an informer in the usual way : the two things on which he based his self-respect were that he had never used violence and had never grassed. Pinky grew vituperative on the subject of snouts, particularly as before the War he had once gone down for seven years after being turned in by a discarded girl-friend. Newcombe had fostered a friendship with the little man in which he never asked questions but talked generally of such and such a job where a nightwatchman had got his skull fractured, or an old-age pensioner had had his ribs kicked in for a few quid, and Pinky's eyes would flash, and sometimes, a little later, he would casually mention some bully boy or other who had come into gelt, and was using it to buy ten-bob whiskies in the afternoon rat-traps.

Pinky worked mostly as a tout, slipping club cards into the palms of the well-fed and prosperous coming excitedly out of the Motor Show or looking smug as they emerged from an expense account dinner at Wheeler's. If times were bad he sold newspapers outside the White City, or spieled at street corners. Newcombe also knew of his rôle as the sporty bystander waiting to put down his money in the three-card game on football specials or racetracks, but he never mentioned it; after all, Pinky was pushing seventy, and mugs never learned. He liked Pinky, and he usually enjoyed listening to his stories, but he was not in any mood for them tonight, and neither was Pinky. He had even bought his own beer, which he now sipped delicately as he looked sadly up into Newcombe's eyes.

"I've got nothing for you, Mr Newcombe," he said eventually. Newcombe said nothing. "None of the boys know this geezer, pretty boy with blonde hair. There's a queer out at Greenwich, goes round the clubs : he dyes his hair every bleeding colour, but it wasn't him, he was in lumber last Thursday." Newcombe grunted and glared at a point two inches above Pinky's head. "I'd stake me arms on it not being any of the boys—even the hard cases wouldn't do that. There's a few who would put the boot on a copper, but blind him, Gawd."

"What about Griffen?"

"Griffen? What's Griffen got to do with it? He don't even know Toms."

"What's Griffen been doing?"

"I wouldn't know. I don't even see him. He doesn't go round the clubs, never goes punting, nothing like that. He's a right bastard, all right; anyone working with him would be tight-mouthed about it, even in drink. There's a lot of talk about the heavy boys; you know, the type who fancy themselves, who shoot their mouths off about what they would do to anyone who grassed on them. Griffen never shoots his mouth off about anything. You know what he's like. What I don't like about him is that he just does it: he don't need to get in a temper, work himself up, or anything like that. Maiming a man wouldn't mean anything to him."

"Who works for him?"

"I don't know, anyone could; the layabouts who hang round his club, he could get any of them for a few quid, but if he wanted someone good it wouldn't be any problem, he'd get them—probably never go anywhere near him, but they'd be working for him just the same."

"Yes."

"But it's all a lot of mooley, Mr Newcombe; this isn't Griffen. He's capable of it all right, I wouldn't put nothing past him, but he don't use kids. And you know as well as I do, if Griffen did do anyone he'd make a real job of it, he'd kill them."

"Griffen has a lot of kids at his parties, doesn't he?"

"Birds. He gets his hands on all the little scrubbers in creation. He's a dirty bastard, but he's not queer, he wouldn't have this pretty boy you're looking for up there."

"Griffen knows him all right."

"If you say so."

"He's looking for him."

"If Griffen was looking for him he'd be a bit edgy, he'd be trying to find something to put between himself and Griffen, wouldn't he? At least, he would if he had any eighteenpence. I thought it was a bit funny, this joker driving about with a shotgun up his kilt."

102

"Why's Griffen looking for him?"

Pinky shrugged. "Does it matter? Could be anything—talked out of turn, can't pay a gambling debt, maybe. That's probably it; cashed a bouncer up at Griffen's gaming-room."

"And of course Griffen would let some kid he'd never seen before in his life into his gaming-room to stick him with a stumer cheque. He must do it all the time!"

"I'm only trying to help."

"What's all the act for, Pinky? Somebody been putting their thumb in your ear?"

"You've got no call to laugh at me. I'm an old man, and when you're old your bones don't set as easily as they do when you're a youngster. I've got no time for Griffen, but what good is it going to do me or anyone else to shout the odds about it, and have some yobbo boot my ribs in? What's the point? You want the man who blinded Toms, don't you? I'm telling you it wasn't Griffen, it was this kid; he shot Toms."

Newcombe lit a cigarette and flicked the dead match off the end of his thumb : it skated high above Pinky's head. Newcombe put his huge fist on the table.

"I'm getting fed up with people telling me things I've heard before. Half of London knows who did Toms—this nancy boy, they all say. Any time I ask a question about anyone else it's all a big silence. I'm still asking, Pinky. Griffen's got something to do with this; he was after this gink, wasn't he? Don't give me the tale again about his muscles; if he's that good it's a pity he didn't catch up with him. Is he still after him?"

"I don't know."

"I bet he isn't. He'll be leaving him to us—suits him down to the ground, that does."

"If I knew anything I'd tell you, Mr Newcombe, you know that."

"Pity you bloody don't, then."

Newcombe scowled heavily round the bar, causing some embarrassment to a mild little man in a trilby hat. Pinky tried to keep his pint in front of his face as long as he could. When Newcombe finally brought his gaze back to Pinky he looked at him for a long time.

103

"How long have you worked for Griffen?"

"Me?" said Pinky.

"Yes, you."

"I swear—"

"You're lying. Old Compton Street, Pinky."

"Oh."

"You've been turning me on."

"No, no, I haven't, honest I haven't. Look, it was nothing to do with Griffen. Topper Martin asked me—"

"That book-shop is Griffen's."

"I know, I know, but look, listen, Mr Newcombe, I'm an old man. I was working this with Topper. It's the old game."

"I'll listen for a bit before I take you down."

"It had nothing to do with Griffen's dirty books. Topper wanted someone to stand outside; you know how it goes, wait for those who stand looking at the windows. There's a window full of those pin-up films: you know the ones, with the pictures on the carton. There was nothing to it, you just waited until some berk stood there looking at them and went up to him and asked if he wanted a private show. You could ask anything you liked, they always haggled a bit, so long as you didn't go lower than a fiver."

"We'll have this down at the station."

"No, listen, all we did was take them to the room above Topper's club. There was a film on all right for the ones who wouldn't part up until they saw something on the screen. You give them a flash and it looked all right, but it was just one of those strip films you can buy for thirty bob anywhere."

"What about the troublemakers?"

"Pah, most of them just creep out again. The odd one, well, Barney's always handy, ain't he? But this was Topper's deal, Griffen didn't set it up."

"Confidence trick."

"Oh, come on, Mr Newcombe, we were only lifting it off some dirty-minded gits, it serves them right. They don't complain to the police, do they?"

"You're a toe-rag, Pinky, a lousy toe-rag."

"Let me get you another drink, Mr Newcombe. Look, you

104

know me, you know I wouldn't really have anything to do with all that crap, it's unhealthy; and that stuff Griffen does with young birds and all that, and then bleeding the poor sods white afterwards, I'd never feel clean again. But that's all it was, honest, working the ringer on a lot of dirty mugs."

"You must have made a lot of money."

"You wouldn't credit it, we used to take a couple of hundred a day. I only used to get ten bob a touch. Of course, you need a lot of faces, that's why Topper roped me in. You've got to have a new face on the corner when the mugs come out again, just in case."

"Why run, then?"

"We've all got our pride, Mr Newcombe; if I have to root behind a few dustbins now and then I don't want anyone to see me at it, do I?"

"Um, all right, Pinky, I'll wear it for now, but don't get ambitious, will you?"

"Me, Mr Newcombe?"

"Stay in your own league, Pinky."

Newcombe went back to his restless looking round the bar. He heard Pinky get up from the table, but he did not look at him again.

16

MILTON had been to Davies's house before. He noted the usual hallmarks of suburbia; the Dorothy Perkins roses standing up like sentries either side of the crazy-paved path, the green-painted front door with its lozenge-shaped bell-push, and the imitation storm lantern porch light. It was not a bad house, getting on a bit in years, slightly out of date, but built by craftsmen : very much like Davies himself.

Milton examined his tongue carefully in the driving-mirror. It was rather coated. Mrs Davies always asked him about his wife, and whether he was going easy on the beer. Davies must have caused her a bit of trouble in that direction when he had been younger.

He reached round and took up his document-case from the back seat, got out, and walked up the garden path. The front lawn looked a bit ragged.

Mrs Davies opened the door; she smiled with genuine pleasure when she saw him.

"Come in, Arthur, out of this terrible weather. Let me take your coat. There, that's it." She ushered him into the lounge. "How's Mary?"

"She's keeping very well, thanks very much."

"You must bring her round to see us one evening. It can't be very much fun for her with you out every evening."

"I certainly will; she'd love that."

Davies was sprawled out in his armchair, wearing an old cardigan and nursing his corporation. He had his feet up on a coffee table. The coal fire was half-way up the chimney, and, of course, his foul old pipe was hanging down from his eye-tooth as usual. He grinned at Milton, and made a slight movement as if he thought of getting up to greet him. He thought better of it. It was Mrs Davies who pushed a chair forward.

"Well, now, Arthur, you've been a busy boy, I hear. Have you had a lab check on it yet?"

"Yes, sir." He opened up his document case and took out the papers. "There were seven hundred tablets, most amphetamine—oh, and there were some small phials with some colourless stuff in; lysergic acid, the stuff they call L.S.D."

"Hallucinatory drugs." Davies blew an enormous funnel of smoke in the general direction of his chiming clock on its little stand over the fireplace. "Anything else?"

"A small quantity of cocaine and some heroin. They were sealed up in tubes; pretty old, according to the lab boys."

"He wouldn't use those himself, they're his bank balance— better than money in some places, and easier to store. You've done well there."

"It's Pawson really."

"Yes." Davies made a thorough examination of his lounge ceiling. "Pawson's a good lad, a very good lad."

Mrs Davies came in with a tray. Davies moved his feet from the little table with some reluctance to allow her to put it down. No-one said anything while she poured the tea. They all drank in silence. It was a good cup of tea.

Davies knocked out his pipe and heaved himself up in his chair to reach his tobacco pouch from somewhere round his backside. "I'm sorry I haven't any cigarettes in the house, Arthur."

"That's all right," said Milton, getting out his own packet. Mrs Davies shook her head, and he lit up with a sigh of relief. Davies rammed about half an ounce of something black and nasty into his pipe-bowl. Milton cleared his throat.

"I think we might get somewhere on the grave itself. It's fourteen years old, and it's a 'D' number. That means it's a private grave."

"Whose is it?"

"It's a woman, Selina Brockhouse; she was thirty-six when she died."

"Fourteen years ago?"

"That's right."

"What did she die of?"

"Multiple injuries. She was in a car smash in the Brompton Road, and was taken to the Middlesex Hospital. She died soon after she got there. I've got a copy of the death certificate."

"So?"

"I've been up there and had a look at their records. I looked up the incident book at the local station as well. It was on July 17, 1952, about two o'clock in the morning. She was being driven back from a party by her husband. They hit the other car head on. There were three people in the other car, and they were all killed. The Brockhouse car was heavier: her husband was knocked about, but he was all right. They were all taken to the Middlesex Hospital. No-one really knew what had happened. Brockhouse said he couldn't remember anything, but it looked as if he was on the wrong side of the road and moving like hell."

"All water under the bridge, Arthur. This poor woman was killed and buried fourteen years ago: this comedian uses her grave to keep his rubbish in. He picked it out because it looked neglected. Probably watched to see if anyone visited it."

"She had a son, Thomas Derek."

Davies sat up very straight. He took the pipe out of his mouth. "How old?"

"He was eight when she died."

"So—he'd be twenty-two now."

"That's right."

"It could be, Arthur, it could very well be. Using his mother's grave. . . ."

"It would be safer, wouldn't it? And he's not likely to think it's a desecration or anything: this isn't a joker who'd think like that."

"So—Thomas—Tom Brockhouse."

Milton made a vague gesture with his hands. "Of course, it might be a right frost, but it's worth pursuing."

"Oh, we're going to pursue it all right, pursue it for all it's worth : it's the only bloody line that we've got."

"He'll be back for his drugs."

"And you want to wait for him, eh, Arthur? It's not a bad idea; it won't be easy, though."

"I doubt if he would come by day."

"Why not? No, I see : he can't know if the girl's told us or not. He's a night-bird, anyway, isn't he?"

"It's not only us he's running from. Griffen would have more chance of picking him up by day. We could have a watch on during the day, but he's almost certain to come by night."

"It could take too long. We could flush him."

"Could we, sir?"

Davies looked up sharply, but Milton had a perfectly straight face. "What I had in mind," said Davies, "was a release to the Press, nothing big : he'll be a great newspaper-reader. A word to one of Newcombe's mates ought to do it, something about the bird coming up in court."

"I think I'm with you, sir." Milton tried to recite his note as casually as if it was something that had just crossed his mind. " 'The police asked that Jenkins, otherwise Gloria Lamarr, be detained in custody as they believe she could assist them in certain inquiries of a serious nature.' She comes up tomorrow; we could get that in tomorrow's evening editions."

"And if he comes tomorrow night, what then?" Davies interrupted.

Milton took the map out of his document-case. "I got this from the borough surveyor. As it's night I think we can forget about the main gates. They'll be locked, and are nine feet high with spikes on the top. It's a bit too public; the gates are on the main road, and well lit by street-lamps. The cemetery is bordered on these sides by main roads. They meet at the cross-roads, here : at the crossroads itself is an ornamental garden, and behind that is the superintendent's house. The cemetery itself begins here, it goes over twenty-two acres."

"Um, what's this?"

"The chapel, about two hundred yards inside the main gate. It's an asphalt road up to there."

"And here?"

"Shrubbery and lime-trees. They screen the chapel from the main road, and they go all along this wall parallel to the road; there's a lawn and flower-beds in front of them, and then the path. At the end of the wall is a recreation field. I think he'll come in there, on that corner. The fence round the sports ground is much lower, about three feet six; it's very easy to get on to, and it's about the right height if you stand on top of it to reach the top of the wall into the cemetery. I had a look at it; there are some marks on the top that look as if someone has used it already."

"Well, there are no lights in there and you can't put a car in : what have you thought up on that?"

"I've marked the grave, sir; it's the eighth plot from the end of this row."

"I see; no trees, shrubs, or anything near it?"

"Not very near, but it's in line with the group here. We've measured from the plot to this square; it's sixty-four feet."

"What's this square?"

"It's a hut, tool-store, sort of potting shed. The gardeners use it while they're keeping the grass down and tidying up the flower-beds. They put it in the middle of the shrubbery to keep it out of sight."

"All right, you've got an observation point, and it's only twenty yards off, but there are still no lights."

"I thought you might have a word with your friends at Central, sir. I'm told that they've got this gadget; from a submarine."

"The one they use for observing brothels; does everyone know about that thing?"

Milton glanced uneasily at Davies's wife, but she smiled placidly back at him.

"All right, Arthur, it sounds all right. I'll set it up with Central."

"Thank you, sir." He gathered all his papers back into his document-case.

110

"You've had the course, haven't you?"

"Sir?"

"Pistol. I want you armed."

"I shouldn't think he'll be bringing his gun with him, sir."

"Maybe not, but you'll have one. I don't want any encores, Arthur; you'll have a gun, and you'll use it if you have to. I don't want any mistakes. If anyone gets a bullet through them make sure it's the other feller."

"Yes, sir."

"And the car: pick the crew you want, so long as it's on the roster."

"Yes, sir."

17

DAVIES drove himself out to Barnes and parked in the forecourt of a pub opposite the small block of flats in which Griffen lived. He stood on the pavement for some time examining it before he crossed the road. It was very well-kept; all the windows were clean, there were no children and no washing-lines. The small lawn at the front was shaved to within an inch of its roots, the concrete forecourt newly swept.

Davies went through the heavy glass doors into the un-cluttered foyer. There was a porter's small desk, but no-one stood there, and Davies read the board, which told him that Flats 7 to 14 were on the second floor. He ignored the lift and took his time going up the stairs. He saw no-one. On the first floor he heard, faintly, the strains of a radio murmuring behind one of the blank mahogany doors. Everywhere the parquet floors gleamed from their waxing; nowhere was there so much as a discarded cigarette packet.

The second floor was a replica of the first, the door to Flat 9 revealing itself only by a brass plate let into the exact centre of the door. Davies detected below this a minute hole which he recognized as the exit-point of a miniature peep-hole; on the other side of the door would be the magnification equipment with which to view the corridor. He was tempted to place his thumb across the lens, but instead, depressed the bell-push and waited. He waited some three minutes before he pressed it again, and this time he heard a faint shuffling. The door was opened by a woman who looked like a housewife.

She was dressed drably, and about her was an air of weary depression. Davies was very surprised.

"Yes?" said the woman.

"Detective Superintendent Davies."

The woman opened the door wider and stood back to allow him to enter. Opposite the front door an inner door stood open, and Davies went through this into a large room overlooking the forecourt of the block. The room seemed to be furnished entirely with settees and armchairs, except for an ornate bar which was built against the far wall. Griffen was standing at the bar, and he watched Davies come in without expression.

Griffen wore the dark grey trousers of a very good suit, with a cream shirt in heavy silk. The shirt collar was open, and he had not shaved. He continued to look at Davies as he lit himself a cigar. Davies sat himself, uninvited, at one end of a settee in dimpled black leather. He took out his pouch and placidly returned Griffen's gaze as he pressed tobacco into his pipe-bowl.

Griffen poured part of a bottle of stout into a huge crystal goblet, and on top of it emptied the remains of a bottle of Dom Perignon. He did not offer Davies anything.

He carried his drink over to a swivel armchair, sat down, and drank deeply from his black velvet concoction. Davies examined him with some curiosity; he had not seen Griffen for a long time, and he was slightly dismayed to find that, although three years older, Griffen was wearing better than himself.

By any standards Griffen was a formidable man: six feet four inches tall, and built to size. Thick black hair furred the back of his huge hands, the fingers of which were nearly an inch across at their base. His face was florid, but strong-jawed and well-shaped; a small scar extended upward from the corner of his mouth. A face, in fact, that could have been hewn out of granite. In one sense an ageless face, but in another the face of middle age, and not that of a man nearing sixty. The only real sign of age was the iron-grey hair that started about an inch above his eyebrows.

H   113

Griffen finished his drink and threw the glass on to a settee; he swung his chair until he faced Davies directly.

"Well?"

"Well, Griffen?"

"Get on with it."

"I've had a man shot, Constable Toms; you'll have heard of it."

"Well?"

"It was done by a friend of yours."

"Talk sense."

"There's only the two of us here. Don't get worried."

"Who's worried?"

"He'll know all about you, Griffen, this feller. He knocked off a scrubber of yours, Gloria Lamarr, and you didn't like it. You wouldn't, would you?"

Griffen scowled. "What the bloody hell do you want, Davies?"

"His name."

Griffen grinned savagely. "Why don't you ask this Lamarr tart?" The question hung in the air.

Davies puffed his pipe for a while in silence. "You've had your hounds out for him, but I want him more than you do, Griffen, and I'm going to have him."

"I don't have to worry, then, do I?"

"What's his name?" Griffen said nothing. "Don't tell me there's honour among thieves."

"You're getting on my wick."

"What's the matter, Griffen? You wouldn't think twice about booting his head in—why not the name?"

"I'll give you what I've always given coppers . . . nothing."

"No-one's too big, you know, Griffen. You're getting an old man, like me. You might want to go somewhere quiet one of these days. You might want us to leave you alone."

"Why don't you start crawling round the room and have done with it? You've tried everything else. What you frightened of, your pension? They going to dock it or something if you don't bring him in?"

Davies's neck went scarlet. "For Christ's sake, Griffen, what

114

sort of rubbish are you made of? He's done it once for no reason, he's going to do it again, to anyone, to a man with a family, to a woman, a kid. Someone decent."

"Oh, someone decent; and who the hell's that?"

"The public, the people everyone else lives on, the people who make things, work all day, week in, week out, pay mortgages, raise their kids. . . ."

"Oh, that lot, the little people. Go down Dean Street, Davies, and you'll see them queueing up for the strip clubs. They can't wait to see things like that Lamarr scrubber stand up and take her clothes off. The public!" Griffen paused and carefully spat his cigar out on to the carpet an inch or so in front of Davies's feet.

Davies clenched his right fist hard inside his jacket pocket. His eyes locked with Griffen's in an endless moment of mutual hatred. It continued through the sounding of the door-bell. The woman came back into the room. Griffen turned his gaze from Davies and looked sourly at the woman. He nodded. The woman looked at him with a curious expression on her face for almost a minute, and then, quite suddenly, she turned and was gone.

"Why the hell does she put up with you?" said Davies.

Griffen gave a mirthless smile. "She's my daughter . . . or so she says."

Someone else came into the room; she was blonde and young, a tall girl with excellent carriage, very well dressed, and very beautiful. She went across the room to kiss Griffen's unshaven cheek.

Griffen looked steadily at Davies as he put out his hand and gripped the girl brutally on the thigh. Davies was careful to keep his face blank. He got up from the settee, collected his hat, and walked out of the room. As he opened the front door he heard the girl laughing.

18

THERE was a flash of lightning as Pawson and Milton walked out along the neat little sanded path to the hut. Almost immediately thunder cracked out above them, as loud as all the hammers of hell. The hut smelled dankly of earth and rust. As Milton pulled the door shut the rain increased in force and began to hit the asphalted roof with the violence of shell-fire. They stood inside in total darkness for a moment or two before Pawson switched on his torch and showed him how he had arranged the little bench by the window, the mounted nightscope, sandwich box, vacuum flask, and personal radio set. Then they were again in darkness, and it was with some bitterness that Milton felt an insidious dampness creep up his legs from the concrete floor. He could feel the sliminess of the mud from beneath his shoes as he felt his way towards one of the boxes in front of the bench. He bumped into Pawson, who was doing the same thing. The revolver at his waistband got in the way, and he took it out and put it in the outside pocket of his overcoat. Then he bent over the nightscope and peered through the eyepieces. It was strange to see the sanded path spring into sight again, this time as if in a deepening twilight. He could see the rain slanting down and hitting the path, and he could very easily read the inscription on the headstone. "Selina Brockhouse, 1916-1952, beloved wife and mother." Pawson cleared his throat.

"Shall I call up the car, Sergeant?"

"No, I'll do it, lad."

He put in the earpiece and pressed the button. There was a screech of static. "Purple 3 to Bandit 4, over."

"Bandit 4 here, am hearing you loud and clear, over."

"There's a hell of a lot of interference."

"It's the storm, Sergeant, build-up of static."

"I know what it is. We're on watch, observation clear. Anything to report?"

"Nothing in sight. Only one car gone by, a large saloon with five or six passengers. Nothing else in sight."

"All right, over and out."

He switched off the set and they sat in silence until Milton began to believe that they had been there for an eternity. He struck a match to look at his watch; they had been there for fifteen minutes. He gave Pawson a cigarette: the dampness coming up from the floor had numbed his feet up to the ankles. He felt unutterably miserable.

Pawson grunted, and there came a wild creaking from his direction.

"What's up?"

"Sorry, Sarge, I've got the cramp."

"Christ."

"I should have got a heater in here."

"Go up on your toes, push your weight down on them—you can sometimes get the knot out."

Pawson subsided.

"Who'd be a copper?" said Milton.

Pawson grunted.

The rain seemed to be heavier. Milton stamped his feet; it did not do much good.

"What a hole."

"It's not too bad in the summer, with the trees out; peaceful."

"You know this place?"

"My father's buried here."

"Let's have some coffee," said Milton.

Pawson poured it out. It was very hot.

"Do you want a sandwich, Sarge?"

"What are they?"

117

"Cheese."

"No."

"I don't blame you," said Pawson.

"How long have we been here?"

Pawson flashed a torch on his watch. "Ten to twelve." They sat without speaking for some time. Milton went off into another of his reveries. It was cut short by the high-pitched call-signal sounding out on the radio. He heard Pawson sit up with a jerk. Milton depressed the speaking-button.

"Purple 3."

"Purple 3, this is Bandit 4. A man has crossed the main road. He's on foot, and is now passing the cemetery gates."

"Alone?"

"Yes, he's wearing an oilskin and a cap. He's looking through the gates; now he's moving on. He's looking about the street. Now moving out of range of the street-lamp." There was a pause, then: "He hasn't appeared beyond the end of the wall. He's gone."

"Right, Bandit 4, keep listening."

Milton snapped his fingers to Pawson and bent over the nightscope. The sanded path sprang again into sight, although this time not so clearly; but the grave could still be seen. The rain beat down with great ferocity, blotting out all other sound. Pawson stood very close to him, peering at his watch; three minutes to climb over the wall and to move through the graves in direct line; five minutes with caution and no visibility. Milton peered intently at the grave. He detected a movement from beyond the focus of the viewing instrument. It came from the rear of the first line of graves.

"Here he comes," said Milton.

He came clumsily, placing his hands on alternate headstones as a guide to his path. He was half crouched against the force of the rain, and it was impossible to judge his height or age. He wore a billowing oilskin and a flat cloth cap, black with the rain. Milton watched him come through the graves and stumble blindly on to the path. When he had reached it he turned back.

118

"There's a light," said Pawson. "He's using a torch to find the grave."

"All right," said Milton. He rose from the nightscope and stood for a moment to adjust his sight to the sudden darkness. Pawson handed him one of the big torches. They left the hut. The wind and the rain struck them violently in the face. They moved on into the empty blackness. They could hear nothing over the sound of the rain as they moved cautiously through the drenched shrubbery towards the path. They moved forward slowly until they could see the light from the torch. It moved waveringly as the boy plunged his hand into the corner of the grave.

Milton switched on his own torch. The boy spun round, and there was a glimpse of a white, shocked face. The cap was very low across his forehead; his eyes screwed up against the light. The oilskin gaped widely at the neck. Almost at once he dipped his head again and ran. Milton shouted, but his words were lost on the wind. The boy kept to the path, running towards the chapel. Pawson outdistanced Milton. Milton angled his torch beam down to the boy's feet to help Pawson. The boy was wearing basketball boots; he cut across the grass verge, his oilskin billowing out behind him; he was running well now that he was on the asphalted road; Pawson was very close behind him. Milton followed them across the grass verge: he was almost over when his boot struck the cornerpiece of a tomb-cover and he went headlong on to the asphalt at the edge of the grass. He swore savagely. He got painfully to his feet; his left leg hurt badly. It took him some time to find his torch again. His overcoat was slimy with mud. He felt for the revolver, which had twisted in the lining of his pocket; the hammer tongue had torn a hole in the cloth, and he had some difficulty in extricating it. He felt gingerly down his left leg, and found that his trouser-leg had been torn open to the knee.

He moved painfully forward to the chapel. He listened carefully, but could hear nothing over the sound of the rain lashing against its walls. He flashed his torch, but the archway was empty. He put out the torch and moved through the archway.

As he reached the far side he heard, from somewhere in front of him, the shrill note of a police whistle. Above the wind came the sound of two shots in quick succession. Milton wrenched the revolver out of his overcoat and ran forward into the darkness.

He shone his torch frantically in all directions as he ran, but everywhere he looked he could see only the drenched surface of the road. As the road curved he could see the lights from the main road ahead of him, and the big iron gates. He ran faster; someone was silhouetted against the gates. When he got nearer he saw that it was Pawson; above him, from one of the spikes, hung a black oilskin. Pawson leaned wearily against the gates. He had lost his hat, and his saturated hair hung across his forehead like that of a medieval cleric. As he reached him Milton saw, with furious dismay, that his right sleeve was ripped to the elbow. Pawson was trying to support the arm with his left hand.

"What the bloody hell happened?"

"He got over," said Pawson, his voice faint. "I caught his coat."

"Did he shoot you?"

"No, caught it—on the spike." He indicated with his head and swayed farther towards the gate.

"Pawson, for Christ's sake!"

Pawson was very pale. The pupils of his eyes were dilated, and he hardly blinked at the light of the torch. Milton directed the beam closely to Pawson's arm; the raincoat and jacket sleeves were ripped almost to the elbow, and blood welled up from the torn flesh along the forearm. The blood was brilliant, and the amount enormous. Pawson began to fall; he slipped slowly past Milton's arm to sit gently in a puddle near the gate pillar.

Milton tore off his sodden overcoat, pulled Pawson out of the puddle and on to the coat. He leaned his head against the gate pillar, tore off his tie, and tied a tourniquet above Pawson's elbow. The rain was pitiless. His leg ached badly. When he rose he had to help himself up by holding on to the gates. A cold sweat joined the rain coursing down his spine. He looked out on to the empty street and shouted. When he looked down again Pawson's head had slumped down on to his chest.

Milton moved away from the gate, stumbling across the grass and flower-beds that bordered the wall.

He had to move Pawson to find the key to the gates. He had some difficulty in pulling the chain and padlock through the interlacing ironwork. He worked out the bolt, and went out into the street. It was completely empty. Away towards the corner near the traffic lights, was a telephone box. He began a jog-trot towards it, cursing bitterly and thoroughly as he did so.

When he was little more than a dozen yards from the kiosk a car lurched round the corner in a racing turn. The headlights were fully up, and Milton was dazzled when they hit him. The car braked sharply and stopped by him, its tyres scraping the kerb.

Milton waited in frozen momentum for some new disaster, but the boots that came across the pavement to him belonged to the patrol crew.

"Sergeant?"

"An ambulance."

"Did. . . ?"

"A bloody ambulance. Pawson—get the poor sod to hospital."

Milton went back with the driver to Pawson : he had slipped down, so that he had sprawled half on his side, his head in a puddle. They carried him out into the light and propped him up in the back of the car. He was breathing all right, but he was very pale and very cold. He moaned a little as they lifted him in. The other constable was listening intently to the radio handset. They made room for Milton in the front seat. He became conscious, for the first time, of the water dripping from every possible part of his body.

"Well?" said Milton.

"We saw him come over," said the driver. "Jumped off the top like a ferret : your man had his coat, but he came out of it. Jeff—Constable Hendrie—went after him. I had to turn the car."

"I heard two shots."

"They were at me," said Hendrie, who was next to Milton. "He was still crouched down, staggering a bit, when he saw me, and he ran straight across the road up towards the traffic lights. I was making on him a bit, and he suddenly turned with this gun in his hand and let off a couple."

"Then?"

"I threw my truncheon at him and he was round the corner."

"I'd got the car up there by then," continued the driver, "and we went round the corner after him. We saw him on the far side of the ride going into an alley. It's a footpath between two shops, and leads into a car-park. We went after him on foot."

"And?"

"There was nothing there."

"Nothing?"

"Nothing at all, Sergeant," said Hendrie. "There wasn't a car, or we would have heard it. It's a pretty long road on the other side of that car-park, but there wasn't a thing in sight."

"Gardens?"

"None; one side there's a high wall, and on the other there's nothing but the backs of shops. He must be holed up in one."

"Bicycle," said Milton, "he used a bloody bicycle." He closed his eyes to clear them of the rain dripping down from his forehead. The call-signal sounded on the handset, and at the same time lights blazed into the car from behind. Milton opened the door and swung his feet out again into the pelting rain: the ambulance men were already climbing down.

Milton opened the rear door of the car. Pawson was leaning back in the corner, and it was awkward to pull him forward without getting hold of his arms. The driver of the patrol car got out and opened the other rear door: he put his arms round Pawson's body and gently lifted him out. The ambulance men laid him down on their stretcher and carried him round to the back of the ambulance. Milton stood in the rain and watched them. As they were loading Pawson another police car—this time a big Westminster—swung past both vehicles

122

and braked heavily to a stop, its bonnet heaving over the pavement. Milton moved towards it, but before he got there Davies swung the passenger door open and got out. He thumped his feet on the pavement and glared at Milton.

"Pawson?"

"They've just loaded him in, sir."

"And?"

"I don't know, sir. The car boys went after him but he cut up an alley. They couldn't catch up with him. He had a bicycle, I reckon."

"Can't they run?"

"He had a gun, sir."

"So did you."

"I was inside the cemetery."

Davies uttered three crisp obscenities and stormed past Milton to the rear of the ambulance. Milton leaned against the patrol car. Constable Hendrie wound down the window and blinked up at him through the rain.

"I've told them to look out for a cyclist, Sergeant."

Milton nodded. Davies shouted for him from the rear of the ambulance. He found to his surprise that as he moved towards him he was limping and sharp daggers of pain darted about in his left leg.

"Get in, Milton, you're going with him, and get them to fix you up as well."

"I'm all right, sir. It's my ankle, that's all."

"You look bloody awful, get in."

Milton got in; the ambulance man followed him. They sat on the seat facing Pawson's stretcher. Milton looked back at the bulldog face of Davies. "I'm sorry it was a balls-up, sir."

Davies grunted, and the door closed. Milton sat back and closed his eyes. He felt the ambulance move into gear and away. He opened his eyes again as they moved off. In the blue interior light Pawson looked terribly like a dead man. The ambulance man said nothing. Milton closed his eyes again and settled down to curse savagely and thoroughly all lay-abouts, tea-leaves, drug-addicts, gamblers, Brockhouse, Griffen, Carter, and Davies, but most of all, himself.

19

AT the hospital the house surgeon on duty spent a long time with Pawson while Milton sat in a little reception cubicle. Very soon after he had arrived two nurses had come in to give him a cup of tea; a reaction had set in when they had removed his right shoe; a warm rush of blood the length of his spine ended in a warmly welcome darkness. He came to, vaguely aware of hands moving about him. His gaze focused on a coloured nurse who was removing his sodden clothing. Then the blankets came round him, and for the first time Milton realized how cold and uncomfortable he had been. The blankets cocooned him like warm cotton-wool.

He fought hard against the desire to sleep. He was able to rescue his cigarettes, damp and crushed in their broken packet. He sat huddled in his blankets and puffing his cigarettes. In all the twenty years since he had first walked, selfconsciously, out on to a beat Milton had rarely been so depressed. He had failed to get evidence before, failed to make arrests before; uncountable times he had known who had done a job, where the criminal had known that he knew, but where there was no proof. It was all in the game: something to dismiss with a shrug, nothing to get cynical about. It evened itself out in the long run.

This was different. He could not remember a man he had wanted more. In bitter self-analysis he realized the mistake he had made; all the time, at the back of his mind, had been the idea that he was pitting his twenty years' experience against an amateur. He realized, with painful clarity, that he had taken it for granted that he would bring him in. It had never crossed his mind that he would fail.

He had made an incredible mistake in not bringing in at least one of the car crew to the wall fronting the road. It was not a mistake he would make again, but that was no consolation to Pawson lying somewhere beyond the cubicle partition with half his arm ripped away, needing God alone knew how many pints of blood to be pumped back into him. The icy thought suddenly came to Milton that Pawson could possibly lose his arm, and every muscle in his body started forth in iron-hard horror. He was still tensed when the house surgeon came to him.

The house surgeon was a young man with dark, wavy hair falling about his forehead. His face was strained white, and his eyes sunk deeply in their sockets. He had probably been on duty all day, only to be raked out of bed after an hour's sleep. Milton knew how he felt.

"How is he, Doctor?"

The doctor made a vague gesture. "He's lost a lot of blood."

"There's no question of any permanent damage?"

"It's too early—Sergeant, is it?"

"Yes."

"I was told you were both policemen." In spite of himself the doctor was forced into a gigantic yawn. "All I can tell you is that he has lost a great deal of blood. The veins—I've closed the wound. The tourniquet made a great difference. He's young and strong—I hope, I think it'll be all right."

"Thank you, Doctor."

"Now." He bent over Milton. One of the nurses came into the cubicle to help him.

"It's just my ankle, Doctor. I tripped, that's all. It's only a bruise."

"Um." The doctor moved the ankle, making Milton grit his teeth. "It's sprained." The nurse produced a bandage, and the doctor bound up the foot and ankle very skilfully, but with the air of a man walking in his sleep.

"Could I see Mr Pawson, Doctor?"

"There wouldn't be any point, he's sleeping. He needs rest,

rest most of all, rest and new blood. Perhaps tomorrow." He finished with Milton's foot and stood up. "You'll be all right." He turned towards the door and yawned again.

"I don't need to stay, do I?" asked Milton. "I can move on it."

The nurse took over, "Not tonight you can't—your clothes are absolutely sopping. You can go home in the morning."

Milton swore savagely beneath his breath. He turned to argue with the nurse, but the blanket fell away, leaving him naked, and he felt ridiculous. He still grumbled when the nurse showed him into a small reception ward, but he got into the bed.

The blue service light near his bed irritated him, and he slept badly.

20

IT was a sardonic Newcombe that arrived the next morning. He went first to see Pawson, and then, towering over a tiny Irish nurse, was led in to see Milton. Poor Milton was sitting on the edge of his bed looking like some sort of refugee. His eyes were bloodshot, his suit was streaked with dried mud, the knee of his left trouser-leg was ripped out, and one of his filthy shoes could not be laced because of his bandaged ankle. Beside him on the bed was a brown paper parcel containing his ruined overcoat.

Newcombe's lip curled. "I've been to see Pawson."

"How is he?"

Newcombe shrugged. "It looks like he'll be all right."

"Good."

"How about you?"

"Just the ankle, Henry. You've heard all about it, I suppose?"

"I heard a bit."

"How's Mr Davies?"

Newcombe sucked his teeth reflectively. "He's not happy."

"No, it'll never be forgotten, will it, the ricket I've made of this lot?"

"Davies okayed it."

"A fat lot of difference that'll make."

Newcombe spat out a piece of matchstick. "Get up, then, I've got better things to do than listen to you being sorry for yourself."

Milton's face flushed and he got up abruptly. He followed

Newcombe out to the old Austin. He did not speak until he was being driven out of the hospital gates.

"Thanks for collecting me, anyway."

"It was Davies who asked me to find out how Pawson was doing."

Milton turned his face to the side window and scowled heavily in turn at a milkman, a constable on point duty, and two middle-aged women with shopping baskets who teetered dangerously on the kerb at the corner of the road as they gossiped.

"Well, be your age," said Newcombe, "you're too old to sulk, for Christ's sake."

"What's up now?"

"You've got a face like a ferret with the mange."

"Let me out at the corner and I'll bloody walk."

Newcombe ignored him. "No bloody commonsense, that's your trouble, no eighteenpence. What did you expect, a round of applause? You take a patrol car, Pawson, trick binoculars, personal radios, and Gawd knows what else, and you screw it. The one way he had to go if he runs and you leave it open—didn't even think of it, did you? Didn't think he'd run? Bighead, too full of how it would look in the report."

"Give it a rest, for God's sake."

". . . so Pawson has to cop it."

"You enjoying this?"

"Well, someone ought to tell you, and Davies won't."

"What's the point, what's the bloody point? I'm a charley; all right, I ballsed it up; I had all the time in the world, and I muffed it. He had me over."

"You still don't get it, do you?" said Newcombe, cutting in on a Mini and scaring its blonde driver out of a year's growth. "I told you myself what that bird said, but you wouldn't listen. You have to go haring off to the boneyard."

Milton was completely bewildered. "What the hell are you talking about?"

"The school!" Newcombe shouted it so loudly a man on the far pavement turned his head round to peer at them. "The college, the bloody university!"

Milton was silent. It was true, he had forgotten. If the boy's name really was Brockhouse, it was almost too easy, perhaps no more than a phone call. He cursed bitterly and thoroughly.

"That's better," said Newcombe.

"What a bloody fool!"

"That's right."

"Where are you driving, Henry?"

"Where the hell do you think? The station, I'm clocking off."

"Let me out, I'm going home for another suit, something for calling on professors."

"Keen, ain't you!" Newcombe sneered, but he swung the wheel.

21

MR GRIMALDI was very unlike Milton's idea of a university don. Small and dapper, he was wearing a very well-cut grey suit with pointed suede shoes and a blue silk shirt. His black, flat hair and pencil-thin moustache showed no grey. His well-nourished face and quick dark eyes gave an impression of action rather than contemplation. Milton could think of half a dozen used-car dealers who bore a family resemblance to him.

"I'm Detective Sergeant Milton, Mr Grimaldi, and I understand that you can help me with some inquiries I'm making."

"Yes," said Mr Grimaldi. "I'm sure you won't mind my asking, but I believe that plainclothes policemen carry cards of identity with them."

Milton opened out his warrant-card and Grimaldi smiled, showing small, even, and very white teeth. He flicked his hand to the chair at Milton's right, and seated himself in a tub swivel chair at the writing-table. He crossed one well-creased trouser leg over the other, and once Milton had sat down shot his cuffs and placed both elbows on the table, raised the tips of his fingers to his chin, and gave Milton a very thorough examination, as if he were filing him away for future reference.

"How can I assist you in your inquiries, Sergeant Milton?"

"I understand that Thomas Derek Brockhouse was a student of yours."

"That is correct."

"When did you last see him, sir?"

"He left some months ago. I have not seen him since."

"Have you any idea where he went?"

"No."

"Would any of the other students know, do you think? Any friends of his? It's very important that we make contact with him."

"Why?"

Milton sighed. "We make inquiries for a number of reasons, Mr Grimaldi. Did Mr Brockhouse finish his course with you?"

Grimaldi gave a quick, tight smile which revealed one-sixteenth of an inch of white teeth. "As I'm sure you are already aware, Sergeant Milton, Mr Brockhouse was sent down from this university."

"I did not know that."

"Not from the Dean's office?"

"They only said that you would tell me anything I wished to know. Why was he sent down?"

Grimaldi gave Milton another unblinking examination before he replied, "His work was not satisfactory. At the end, he was not at all satisfactory."

"As his tutor, you would have seen a lot of him, sir, he would have come to see you very often?"

"Yes, he came very often. He always sat in the chair you are sitting in, Sergeant."

"You would have spoken to him about his work—why it was unsatisfactory, I mean?"

"I knew why it was unsatisfactory."

"Would you mind telling me?"

"A university is thought of, by those who do not enter one, as a rather cloistered establishment. A place of dreamers, a place of quiet study. Would you think of a university as such a place as that, Sergeant?"

"Yes, I suppose I would."

"A university is a pressure chamber. Bright little boys and girls come along every year with their bright little shiny faces. They come in all shapes and sizes and from all sorts of places, they come with all sorts of ideas, but there is always one thing that they never think of, never dream could possibly happen—failure."

"Yes," said Milton.

"They have been told so often that they are so clever, you see; they have been the cleverest boy in the school, the girl who carried off all the prizes, the favourite of their day school teachers, the one child, perhaps, of a big family who is going on to university while all the others go out to work. Do you understand?"

"I believe so."

"They have never failed before. Everything they have done, even when they have only half-tried, has always been applauded. They have got used to success, but when they come here they find that to be intelligent is commonplace; to be the best among the best is a challenge they have never had to face because before they have always been the best. It is not at all rare, Sergeant, for students to commit suicide if they fail their degree."

"And Brockhouse?"

Grimaldi smiled. He took an elegant black case from his pocket and extracted a thin cheroot. He took his time lighting it; he did not offer one to Milton.

"I thought you only wanted to trace Mr Brockhouse's whereabouts."

"I also want to know anything else I can about him. Would you say he was one of those who was not clever enough?"

"No, I would not say that." He blew a perfect smoke-ring and watched it lazily disintegrate in front of him. "He was very intelligent." He looked at Milton with some distaste. "It was his concentration that was at fault: he was distracted very easily. It was a question of patience."

"You mean he couldn't wait for results?"

"No, I don't think I mean that at all."

"I'm sorry to appear dense, Mr Grimaldi."

"He did not spend more than a small amount of time on his studies. His essays were always written minutes before they were due. He took no notes at lectures. His reading was rarely what he required to take his degree. He was not interested in taking his degree. It was not what he was looking for."

"What was he looking for?"

132

"Something in which he could see some point. He was unable to find it."

"I don't understand this," said Milton. "Was it something he wanted to do or to be? Do you mean he did not know what he wanted to do for a living when he left here?"

Grimaldi gave a very tiny sigh. "What is it that gives point to your life, Sergeant? No, allow me; you believe in your job, I think, though at times you no doubt dislike it, but you feel it is a job that must be done if people are to sleep safely in their beds at night. You believe in your family, you had a high regard for your parents, over and above the usual irritations of family life. You have a similar regard for your wife and family—if, of course, you have either. You have certain friends, no doubt other policemen. You have any number of contacts with life through other people, and remembered moments of happiness, holidays, your honeymoon. All these things give point to your life. They are for you the worth-while things."

"Yes," said Milton.

"Thomas Brockhouse did not have those things."

"None of them?"

"None."

"Didn't he have a family?"

"He was an emotional pauper. I doubt if you can envisage what that means. He remembered his mother; he knew that she had been killed by his father. He was told so by his mother's parents; apart from that it was breathed into the very atmosphere of his home, and that is even more deadly. And his mother had not been killed in a dramatic way so that his father could be punished by the law, itself a parent figure. His father had not been punished at all. You see the importance of that? The only one who had been punished was Tom himself. His father was somewhere else in a life from which Tom was excluded."

"I understand that."

"It is easier, of course, if you can believe in God because you can then persuade yourself that it will all change in another world in which justice will truly be done, and deserts equably distributed."

133

"But he didn't believe in God."

"His intelligence did not allow him to believe in God, and from his studies he took the knowledge that he was a miniscule speck clinging, like a cheese-worm, to the outer crust of a minor planet. Indistinguishable at any distance, even from the top of a high building, let alone from the heavens, like any one of the other millions. Even less distinguishable from all the millions who have already lived and died, and whom it was ridiculous to believe lived on. No-one cares now what the dead did when they were alive : whether they were good or bad, clever or stupid, guilty or innocent. It is ridiculous to believe that they are all living somewhere else. And since he knew that after death there was nothing, what does it matter how one lives?"

"What's the point, in fact?"

For the first time Grimaldi gave a genuine smile. "That's right, Sergeant, what is the point?"

Milton closed his notebook. "Do you think he's mad?"

"No, I don't think so, but you might persuade a psychiatrist to say so if he happens to hold a certain theory. In my view there is no question of him being insane. He is simply a badly flawed human being. He has no creative instincts. He despises creation or anything connected with it; happiness, regard of others, codes of morality."

"Why did he leave?"

"I thought I told you."

"You told me he was unsatisfactory, but you also said that he was very intelligent. That doesn't sound as if he failed any examinations."

Grimaldi grinned. "You really are a detective, aren't you, Sergeant? I apologize for forgetting that." He changed his pose and leaned back in his chair to study the ceiling. He held his cheroot with elegance. "There was some trouble." He blew another perfect smoke-ring and pierced it with his cheroot; Milton waited patiently. "A girl student was found in his room : that isn't unusual, of course, it's taken for granted nowadays that that sort of thing happens. You can't cluck around men and women of twenty or so like a mother hen, you have to turn a blind eye. But in this case a blind eye could not be turned; the girl was hysterical."

"Why?"

Grimaldi shrugged. "He attacked her, he would not say why. She had gone up to his room willingly enough, she had been there plenty of times before, but this time she either did something or said something that sent him berserk. She was on the floor and he was kicking her when the others came to find what all the noise was about. When they pulled him away from her he tried to attack them with a knife."

"Was he charged?"

"No."

"Why not?"

"We prefer to deal with our problems in our own way if we can. He did not injure anyone with the knife. Fortunately, the first man in was a Rugby player, and he took it away from him without any trouble at all, apart from a small hole ripped in the sleeve of his jacket."

"And the girl?"

"There is no question that he used the knife on her. She had a black eye and a number of bruises on her body, but there was no real damage. She was more shocked than anything else."

"What was her name?"

Grimaldi did not reply immediately. "I don't think I can tell you that."

"Why not?"

"She begged us not to inform the police at the time : to do so now would be a breach of confidence."

"And you think that that is more important than a man like this walking about free? To do it to someone else?"

"I'm not trying to be obstructive. The girl is no longer in this country. She did not want to talk to the police at the time; she would hardly want to now. In any case, she hasn't seen him since that night. How could she help you?"

"No-one knows until we've asked her."

"I gave my word."

"All right. Where did Brockhouse live?"

"He had lodgings, a room; he left that when he left university."

"To go where?"

Grimaldi shrugged.

"There must be some sort of address. He must have come from somewhere."

Grimaldi gave some time to an examination of his fingernails. "There is the address from his enrolment, somewhere north. Perhaps the bursar's office. . . ."

"Thank you." Milton got up. His leg had stiffened while he had been sitting, and his limp became heavy as he moved towards the door. "I'm sorry to have kept you so long."

"It has been a fascinating experience, Sergeant."

He carefully blew a perfect smoke-ring in Milton's direction before he closed the door.

22

IT was late in the afternoon when Milton got back to the station. He was glad to get there : he was feeling the effect of his uncomfortable night in hospital and the strain of favouring his sprained ankle.

Newcombe had not yet come on duty. The day sergeant told him that Davies was in but did not want any visitors. Milton went in to the C.I.D. office; both his desk and Pawson's were piled high with crime reports and circulars. He put his left leg up on Pawson's chair and rang through to Davies.

"Milton, sir."

"I'm busy."

"I would like to see you, sir; I think I have something useful."

"I'll call you," said Davies, and slammed the phone down.

Milton cursed; it meant that he had to stay in the station. He picked up one or two of the crime reports and threw them back again : he was not in the mood. He took his leg gingerly off the chair and lowered it. The blood was pulsating through his ankle as if it were trying to force the bones apart. He limped out to the reception area again. The day sergeant watched him emerge from his door with a blank expression.

"I'm going up to the canteen," Milton told him. "Mr Davies might call me."

"I'll take a message."

"Thanks," said Milton. The day sergeant continued to look at him without any interest at all, and as Milton went on up the corridor towards the canteen he missed Newcombe.

The canteen was empty except for a car crew taking a break. Milton bought his tea and carried it over to a table facing the door. He felt lonely. His tea was stewed, and one of his headaches was starting. He took out his cigarettes, and found that he was out of matches. To cheer himself up he took out his notebook and turned up the page on to which he had copied the entry from the bursar's office. "H. E. Mitchell, Moat Farm, Tinelthrope, nr Culverton, Salop."

At last he had a link, however tenuous, with the fair-haired, good-looking, intelligent, and vicious youth who had shot Toms's eyes out. Amid all his discomfort a warmish glow of achievement had started up. It was annoying that he was not able to tell someone. One of the car crew was telling the other a joke, and they both laughed, then they looked at their watches and stood up, scraping their chairs back, and went out. They left the canteen very empty, and after a moment Milton followed them.

When he got back to the reception desk the sergeant was on the phone, and he had to wait while full particulars were written down about somebody's dog.

"Did Mr Davies call?"

"No, but you've got a visitor." He indicated a woman sitting on the bench by the door. It was Sally Carter.

"Hello, Mr Milton."

"Hello, Sally."

"Can I see you for a moment?"

"Of course; come in." He opened the door of the C.I.D. room. He hobbled across to clear the chair in front of his desk. Sally Carter pulled her nylon fur tightly round her before she sat down. Milton sat at his desk and dumped all the papers on it into the wire tray.

"Have you hurt your leg?"

"I knocked it about last night."

"Chasing someone, I suppose?"

"Yes."

"It must be a hard job."

"It has its moments; what did you want to see me about?"

"About Harry."

138

"Yes?"

"He's not a bad man, Mr Milton, not really. He's not vicious. I know he's got a record, I know he's been a fool; this gambling, it's an illness really. . . ."

Milton said nothing.

"You know my shop. It's a good business. I've worked hard for it, like my old dad. He never had a shop of his own. It was the one thing in life that he wanted, but he never got it. I suppose it was because of him that I was determined to have one."

"Yes," said Milton gently.

"Harry wouldn't have had anything to do with the shooting of your policeman, Mr Milton."

"He told you, did he?"

"He told me everything, all of it; all the lies, Griffen, everything. He's realized what he's got himself into."

"Does he know you're here?"

"No, he doesn't know. He'd be ashamed."

"Why are you here, Sally?"

"If Harry goes inside now it'll finish him; you know what it's like. He's had a lot of trouble with his stomach the last year or so, he's had an ulcer. If he goes back into prison now he'll never be the same again. He's worried sick about it."

"What does Griffen say?"

"He hasn't been near Griffen."

"How do you know?"

"He promised."

"Oh, yes."

"I know, I know, he's said it all before, he's told so many lies. But it's different this time, it really is."

Milton leaned back in his chair, carefully easing his foot. "Why is it different?"

"If there's ever a breath of anything ever again I'm finished. I'll leave him. The girls would understand. They're not kids any more. It was different when they were small."

"You said all this the last time."

"He's not done anything for nine years."

139

". . . That we know of. What do you expect us to do, Sally—pat him on the head, tell him to be a good boy?"

"If he had a chance. . . ."

"He's had a few of those."

"He really does mean it this time, Mr Milton. He's not young any more. He didn't steal those cars, he just did them up. It was this gambling, the money he owed, and . . . oh, hell, you know what Harry's like."

"What did you really come to see me about, Sally?"

She settled herself more comfortably in her chair and crossed her legs so that her coat fell open.

"It's that Davies; he's going to work it on Harry, isn't he?"

"Don't be silly."

"You don't think Harry had anything to do with shooting that copper. Harry said you told him."

"That's right, I did tell him. I told him a lot of other things as well; did he tell you about them?"

"Griffen?"

"And the car. He knew who he gave that car to."

"It's still Griffen."

"Harry could identify him."

"How can he? You know what they'd do to him and Jill and me."

"How do you know? Anybody can say anything; one of these days someone is going to identify someone, Griffen or no Griffen. He's not anything new. There's always been a Griffen, and sooner or later they fall. Every time. They always overreach themselves. It's little people who make them feel big, give them a wrong idea of their own importance. Of course Griffen thinks he's big if everyone goes round giving him credit for every punch-up from here to the Mile End Road."

"You'll never touch Griffen."

"Won't we?"

"Well, he's big, isn't he, tons of money and everything else? He knows all the big pots, M.P.'s and bankers. He's protected, isn't he? Once you get in with that lot they stop anyone getting to you. Mess them up proper, wouldn't it, if he got knocked off?"

140

"You know him?"

"I've met him. You can't get to him—leastways, Davies can't, that's why he's going for Harry, and it's a bloody shame. All he did was do up a few cars; so would you if you knew what the alternative was. What harm did Harry do to anyone? If he goes to gaol now it's the end of his life, he'll be ruined."

"Sally, why kid yourself? You know as well as I do that Harry's bent. He's got a crooked streak in him a yard wide. O.K., he likes his family, his kids, and all the rest of it. It didn't stop him from going on the game before, and it won't again. Oh, I know, he's promised, sworn on a stack of Bibles for all I know, and you believe him : he probably believes it himself. It can't seem worth it where he is now, between us and Griffen. If he manages to get out of this he'll be all right, for a time, and then the itch will start up again and he won't be able to resist it. He'll start again, just in a very small way, and there won't seem to be any harm in it. He'll gamble and lose and won't be able to pay and be frightened to tell you. It'll be the same old tale all over again. Except he'll be a little more cunning. He'll fool you all the way, and then, when we come for him again, you'll be there calling us all the bastards under the sun, just like last week. He's no good, he never will be, and you're too good for him."

Sally Carter got up and wrapped the coat carefully round her body. "That's it, then, he's going inside."

"I didn't say that. It's early days. Our main job is to find the boy wonder Harry gave the car to, and when we get him"—Milton shrugged—"we may not need Harry at all. I don't think we will, because it's ten to one this joker will want to shoot it out. So what I'm telling you is not to expect any miracles, whether he goes inside or not."

Sally moved towards the door. "We never know who we're picking, do we?"

"That we don't." Milton got up from his desk and limped forward to open the door.

"Thank you, Mr Milton."

"Any time, Sally."

She moved off into the reception area and out into the

141

street. Milton watched her walk. Her skirt rose above her knees as she stepped up the two stairs to the street door. Her legs were those of a girl. Milton sighed, and turned back towards the C.I.D. room when he heard the thump of unmistakable footsteps. Davies came down the corridor, his overcoat flapping open, trilby squarely on his head, the usual spirals of smoke drifting behind him. He nodded curtly towards Milton.

"Can I have a word with you, sir?"

"I'm late already."

"It's rather important."

"Write a report."

"It's a bit complicated. . . ."

"I said a report." He brushed past Milton and turned again just before he reached the street door. "Have it waiting for me." Then he pushed the door open and was gone. Milton looked after him and cursed savagely, until he became conscious that the desk sergeant was watching him with close interest. Milton scowled at him and retreated into the C.I.D. room.

He went over and uncovered the typewriter on Pawson's desk. He got out his cigarettes, and discovered all over again that he did not have matches. He wound the paper in the typewriter, but found it difficult to start. After a time he began laboriously to tap out the 'officialese' version of his conversation with Grimaldi. As he typed on he became absorbed in trying to create a connected narrative. He plodded on, lost to the world, oblivious now to the throbbing of his left foot, no longer conscious that he was without a smoke.

When he finally raised himself from his anxious crouching over the typewriter there was an acute pain at the back of his neck. He had filled six foolscap pages. He read it through, and was disappointed to find that it read far less persuasively than it had when running through his mind. He signed the last page and got up. His left foot had gone numb, but as he went towards the door it came violently to life; the blood returned to his ankle, and it felt as if someone was holding it across a blowlamp.

When he emerged painfully into the reception area he found

that Newcombe had come on duty. He produced his cigarettes once again. Newcombe took one, and flicked his lighter. Milton inhaled deeply.

"Well?" said Newcombe.

"I saw him, Brockhouse's old teacher. He knew him pretty well."

"And?"

"Says he's a nice feller, likes hurting people, knocks girls about, sticks knives in people. An emotional pauper."

"How much?"

"That's college chat for a right bastard."

"Do they know where he is?"

"Where he came from, Shropshire. He's a country boy." He waved the papers of his report. "It's all here, every bloody word that Davies wouldn't listen to."

"He went to see Pawson."

"He didn't say anything to me about it."

Newcombe grinned. "He must have knocked you off his list after last night."

"What's up? How is Pawson?"

"I don't know, but it can't be all that good. Davies went to see the doctors. Pawson hasn't got anybody."

"Nobody?"

"Well, he's got a girl somewhere, but she's only nineteen. I'd have thought you'd have known that, Arthur."

"We never talked about it."

"He was your boy."

"Well, maybe, but we didn't give each other our family histories. He's only been here three months. Last night was the first time I'd ever been on watch with him."

Newcombe shrugged. "The quacks wanted to talk to somebody."

"That doesn't sound so good. I hope to Christ there's nothing really wrong with him."

"How was he last night?"

"He looked a bit rough when I got to him, and he looked a bit bad in the ambulance, but when I spoke to the doctor last night he more or less said it would be all right."

"Well, you'll know tomorrow; Davies won't keep it to himself."

"Thanks for cheering me up." Milton went on up the corridor to Davies's room and switched on the light. As he was about to lay his report down on the blotting-pad he noticed his own name among the disjointed doodling that Davies had scribbled all over the top sheet of the pad. Davies had written "Milton" in carefully indented block capitals and had then boxed it round on three sides with a close-knit spiral across the top. It was a very neat effort. He scanned the rest of the pad, but there was nothing else that he could connect with himself. Davies's wastepaper-basket was half full of crumpled paper, and Milton was strongly tempted to have a look at what was in it, but instead he shrugged, laid his report down on the blotter, and went out, switching off the light.

When he got back to the reception desk Newcombe was taking a call on the outside line. Milton went back into the C.I.D. room to telephone his wife and let her know that he was on his way home. He put on his hat and coat and went out again.

Newcombe was still on the phone, but he looked up as Milton moved past him towards the entrance door and raised his hand in salute as he went out into the street.

23

MILTON sat hunched on the settee in his living-room staring gloomily at his television screen while his wife sat placidly knitting. Since he had returned from the station he had eaten his steak and kidney pudding, put on his carpet slippers, propped his sprained ankle up on the settee, and had exchanged less than a dozen words with his wife. It was only the second evening he had spent at home since Toms had been shot.

Sometimes when he was on duty during the evenings, especially if he was on a job that was particularly uncomfortable or monotonous, he would look forward to spending an evening at home. Although he always started out with good intentions any conversation always petered out. He seemed to have lost the point of communication with his wife. It always ended up in the same way, with him slumped in front of the fire, not quite asleep, while his wife went on with her endless knitting of something or other for her sister's children. She was very fond of small children.

She had never been interested in his work, and he had long given up telling her of his cases. He thought, as he often had in the past, that it made no real difference to his wife whether he got back in the evenings or not. He found himself thinking of Sally Carter, and he became slightly embarrassed when he realized that he was trying to imagine her sitting at the other end of the sette to him. He tried to clear his mind of all thought, and his eyes began to close as he sank into somnolence.

When the telephone sounded it was as if it came from the

end of a long, muffled tunnel, and he stirred, but he did not come back to consciousness until his wife shook his shoulder.

"Arthur, it's the phone for you."

Milton struggled up. "Davies?"

"No, it's a woman. She won't give her name. I'll tell her you're busy."

"No, no, I'll go." He stretched and moved his left leg gingerly to the floor. It seemed to be easier than it had been. He hobbled out into the hall, and shivered as he picked up the receiver. The hall was freezing.

"Yes?"

"Mr Milton?"

"Yes, who is it?"

"You told me to phone you."

"Who are you?"

"The Lagoon Club."

"I remember." He frantically tried to activate his brain into instant recall. "You know Brockhouse?"

"Who?"

"The one who shot Toms."

"I didn't know that was his name."

"You had something to tell me."

"I don't know anything."

"You know Brockhouse."

"I saw him a couple of times, that's all."

"That will do for a start."

"That was all I meant when I spoke to you."

"Was it?"

"Yes."

"But you wouldn't want me to come down to the club and ask you?"

"No, no, you mustn't do that."

"Tell me, then." The world is full of frightened people.

"I didn't know his name, not what you said. They called him Tom."

"Who did?"

"Topper, Barney, all of them."

"He worked for Griffen?"

146

"He was a collector, he hung on to some, and there was something about a girl. . . ."

"Is Griffen looking for him?"

"I don't know, none of them talk about it." Milton stroked his tongue thoughtfully across the top of his teeth. It sounded all right.

"That's all I know. I swear, I don't know anything else." Milton did not answer, and a note of desperation sounded in the woman's voice. "You won't come down to the club, will you?"

"Not for a pension," said Milton, and replaced the receiver.

He became suddenly aware that the icy draught sweeping up the hall from the front door had chilled the pit of his stomach. He shivered and turned back towards the living-room, but before he was able to turn the door handle the telephone rang again and he went back.

He recognized the voice of the night-duty operator. "Sergeant Milton?"

"Yes."

"I have a call for you, Sergeant; Superintendent Davies."

"Right."

"Milton?"

"Yes, sir."

"I've read your report."

"Yes, sir."

"You're very sure that this is the same joker?"

"I can't see that there can be much doubt about it, sir: once you put together that business of the grave with the girl's story and what we've got from Grimaldi."

"Uh—huh. This address you've got in Shropshire—why do you think that a squad man should go up there? Is that where you think he's hiding?"

"No, I don't think so. The court report on that girl was only in London in the evening papers and he turned up in Ealing the same night. He must be in London, or very near to it. He could have a room anywhere. None of us would know him if we passed him in the street. The only people who would are Griffen's lot, and they're not likely to be hunting him anywhere outside their own patch. No, what I've been thinking about

147

is that gun, the shotgun. He seems pretty used to guns, much more used to them than a city boy is likely to be. It seems to make sense that if he came from a farm, then that's where he first used them, particularly the shotgun. If he did, then someone's likely to remember. The locals would check to see if he was there, and ask if anyone had a London address on him, but they couldn't do much else; no reason why they should. I think a squad man might be luckier, root around, get something worth while."

"And that's all? You're not keeping anything to yourself, are you, Milton?"

"No."

Davies said nothing for some time. "All right," he said finally. He sounded tired. "There could be something in what you say. I'll put it through. But if there isn't anything up there I don't want any frigging about on spec. You come back. You can stay overnight, tomorrow night, but I want you back the day after. Go tomorrow."

"Yes, sir."

"And report."

"Yes, sir."

"Make sure you do." There was a note of finality in his voice.

"Is there any news of Pawson, sir?"

Davies breathed heavily before he answered. "He's better than he was. They've saved his arm."

"I didn't know he—"

"Well, he did. It's been touch and go. The veins in his arm were ripped across, and the tendons. He lost part of the muscle. It looks as though he'll be all right now, but it's likely to be a long job."

"I didn't know, I'm sorry."

"Yes." Davies's breathing was heavy.

"It was my fault, I should have been quicker." Davies said nothing. "He was alone, an amateur, I took it for granted he'd come without trouble. I should have reckoned with him having another gun. I should have brought the car in closer. I should—"

148

Davies either sighed or yawned. "All right, Arthur, it's all true, and I'm not pleased about it, nor is Mr Miller. It's a mark against you, and you know what that means. But bear this in mind; if you had been quicker and crowded him he's likely to have used his gun sooner than he did. Pawson could be dead, and so could you."

"I suppose that's true."

"Then stop thinking about it—there's nothing you can do now. Get up to Shropshire and bring me back a lead."

The receiver crashed down before Milton could give any reply.

24

IT had been a long time since Milton had travelled north. It was intriguing to look into the defenceless rears of the little houses that bordered the line as it unreeled through the suburbs of north-west London. Then, as the houses thinned out, he watched the telephone wires go singing by, and was mildly diverted, as he had been since a boy, by roads running parallel to the line and then moving abruptly off at an angle.

It was not until he was nearing Birmingham that he settled down to think seriously of what he had taken on. He knew that he had put himself in an exposed position in pushing so hard for this trip. Davies, now convinced that he had some special knowledge, would be expecting him to bring back something worth while. Milton found it hard to analyse his reasons for making such a point of tracking Brockhouse to his origins. It would not be clever to go back with the sort of information that could have been picked up by a local bobby. This whole case had been soured from the start, all the way through there had been something unsatisfactory about it: perhaps it was simply that he was past his own youth and could not get inside the mind of this new sort of criminal.

The trouble was that now he was on his way he had no clear idea of what he was going to do. All he had was a vague feeling that there was something up here worth knowing, something to see, to find, something that would draw together the loose ends that had dogged him since the case began. The nagging fear he now had was that he had no idea at all as to what it could be.

He settled back to turn over in his mind the things that he needed to ask when he arrived at Shrewsbury, but the rhythm of the train and the heat pumping out of the ducts beneath his seat were irresistible. He slowly drifted into a sleep from which he was awakened by the brakes of the train as it screeched to a halt in Shrewsbury station.

He emerged from the train rather crumpled, and as he carried his case along the platform his limp became pronounced. He felt like an unsuccessful brush-salesman. Even so, the youngish detective in a sports jacket who was waiting for him had no hesitation in stepping forward as Milton reached the barrier.

"Sergeant Milton?"

"That's right." Milton shook hands.

"Wilson, Detective Constable. I'm your detail, Sergeant, to take you out to the village."

"You know the place?"

"I came from quite near there." He turned towards the exit. "Will you want to go on to the station?"

"What I want," said Milton, "is a bit of refreshment. What time do they open round here?"

"There's a pub across the square; they do sandwiches, pies, that sort of thing. I've got the car just outside; you can leave your case there if you like."

The pub was up a small street, an old-fashioned place with a high mahogany bar and tinted windows which shrouded the interior in a restful amber light. Milton bought two pints of draught bitter and a huge pork pie. They sat at a small iron-legged table at the far end of the bar, which was empty except for four men wearing almost identical tweed suits who seemed to be selling things to each other.

"Well," said Milton, "you know what I'm up here for?"

"Not really, Sergeant. All I know is that you want to go out to the Mitchells' place at Tinelthrope."

"You know them?"

"Not personally; the Mitchells grow wheat and barley

mostly. I've got an aunt and uncle who live just outside the village, and I stayed with them for a time when I was a kid. They never mixed with the big farmers like the Mitchells: but they knew them, knew of them."

"What do they think of them?"

"Good people—the old man, anyway, a very good farmer, very respected man."

"What about his grandson, the son of his daughter, name Tom, do you know him?"

"No, but I wouldn't. It's seventeen, eighteen years ago since I stayed there, and he would have been very small then. My inspector, Mr Gearing, told me that you were interested in him under the name of Brockhouse, so I checked to see if anything was known."

"And is there?"

"Nothing." He watched Milton bite into his pork pie. "He has never been in any sort of trouble as far as I can see; no-one in that family has."

Milton finished his beer and stretched. "How long will it take us to get to this Tinelthrope? Far, is it?"

"It's about twenty-eight miles. We'll do it in well under the hour."

Milton got up. "All right, then."

He waited for Wilson to lead the way, and then followed him back to the car. Wilson manœuvred the car out into the traffic and through the town, which looked to Milton much like any other town. He had never been to Shrewsbury before, and looked about him with interest, but saw only the usual shops and supermarkets, banks, pubs, and the occasional statue of some tame general. Then the houses thinned out and they were finally through the last band of ribbon development: they swung wide of the town, and out into the refreshing panorama of the countryside. Milton enjoyed glimpses of stacked barns, chicken-strewn farmyards, and fields that seemed to stretch as far as the horizon.

"What are those brick buildings?"

"Broiler houses. It's where they breed the chickens for three months with the lights on and automatic feeders; they never see daylight."

"Poor beggars."

They drove on in silence until, after one or two sidelong glances at Milton, Wilson said, "Will you be bringing the boy back, Sergeant?"

"I don't know."

Milton looked at Wilson reflectively. "Would it make it awkward for you locally?" Wilson shrugged. "You needn't worry, it's a million to one he's still in London. I hope his granddad will know where."

"You think he'll say?"

"You know him; you tell me."

Wilson considered this for some time. "The old man's straight as a die, one of the old school, a gentleman, he'd never do anything out of line, but he'd stand up for anyone in his family, especially his grandson. I'd say it depended on what had been done."

"What about blinding a policeman with a shotgun?"

Wilson's head jolted upright. "Is that what he did?"

"We think so."

Wilson drove on at an increased speed, and Milton sat looking at the countryside which he no longer saw. It was another twenty minutes before Wilson spoke again, and then all he said was, "This is Tinelthrope." They moved through a small village, and on its far side swung across a stone-walled bridge and down a narrow hilly road past an old ruined mill. Wilson stopped the car at a five-barred gate set in a thorn hedge.

"This is it," said Wilson. "Moat Farm."

Milton got out of the car and leaned on the gate. About seventy-five yards away, at the end of a sanded drive, was the house. It integrated beautifully into the hill: built of yellow stone and roofed in the old blued slates of some long-closed quarry, it blended into the fields that stretched beyond, with their tracery of distant hedgerows. To the right of the house ranged farm buildings, and between them and the house was a clean-swept yard. He heard Wilson come up behind him. "Shall I come in with you, Sergeant?"

"No. Stay in the car. I'm not expecting any trouble, but if you do hear a shot call your station up before you do anything."

Milton opened the gate and walked slowly up the sanded drive to the house. He breathed deeply, savouring the air like rare wine. When he reached the house he looked for a knocker or bell-push but found neither. He tapped on the door a few times, but without result; he stepped back and walked along the front of the house looking into the rooms, but he could see no-one. When he reached the corner of the house he saw, across the yard, and standing by the farm buildings, a very tall and erect old man holding a walking-stick. He was looking directly at Milton, who shouted across to him, "I am looking for Mr Mitchell." The old man beckoned to him, and Milton went over.

"Who are you?" said the old man in a deep, quiet voice.

"I'm a police officer." Milton took out his warrant card. "Metropolitan Police. What do you want?"

"Are you Mr Mitchell?"

"Yes."

"I understand that you have a grandson, Thomas Derek Brockhouse; is he staying with you?"

"No; why do you want to see my grandson?"

"Could we go inside, Mr Mitchell? There are a number of things I would like to ask you."

The old man looked directly into his eyes for an endless moment before he turned and, with a gesture of great courtesy, indicated to Milton a shed built at one end of the implements barn. Milton stepped to one side to allow the old man to walk ahead of him. Neither spoke as they entered, and the old man went across to a chair against the far wall. He held himself erect, and his face had a power that sometimes appears in the faces of the very old when they have character and their skin has taken on the texture of very old leather. As he sat with both hands resting on the handle of his walking-stick, with his thick white hair framing his magnificent profile, he had great dignity. Milton felt that he was in the presence

154

of a past nobility. The old man sat in profile like the portrait of a long-dead emperor.

Above the old man's head were delicately tinted drawings of mallards, pheasants, and several other birds unknown to Milton. There were also engravings of racehorses taking fences, looking unnatural with all four hocks splayed outward, as they used to be drawn before photography proved that horses ran in sequence. Everything in the shed was very old except an unframed photograph that had been tacked to the wall by the window with panel pins. A badly taken snapshot turning sepia, it was of a young boy of thirteen or so, in jeans, with an open-necked shirt. One hand held up a brace of duck, the other clutched the long barrel of a shotgun. He grinned at the camera with self-conscious charm, his head bent engagingly towards a high left shoulder. His features were attractively regular, and his hair had been bleached by the sun.

Milton examined the snapshot closely for some time, and when he looked up he saw that the old man had turned his head to watch him.

"This is your grandson, isn't it, Mr Mitchell?"

The old man looked at him for some time before he nodded.

"I understand that you would be reluctant to tell me any-thing that you feel might harm him."

"Who understands anything?" said the old man. "I'm seventy-four years old, and I understand less now than I did fifty years ago. Have you any children, Sergeant?"

"No."

"Are you a religious man?"

"Not particularly."

"No-one seems to be these days. It was all so different when I was young: everyone seemed so certain of that sort of thing. No-one had any doubts, or if they did they kept them to them-selves. These days it seems to be the people who believe in God who keep it to themselves. I'm sorry to ramble on, Sergeant; I'm afraid that I am turning into a boring old man."

"I'm not bored."

"You think about the past a lot when you get old. It seems more real to you than the time you live in now. I miss my

155

children, Tom and Selina; they were lovely children. We were complete then. Tom would have had this place, and he would have been a good farmer. Tom would have had the patience. He was very good-natured and clever with his hands. He had a gift with animals, and a lot of ideas. He was always wanting me to increase the stock, and Selina loved life in the country. She was beautiful, my Selina. It's when you're old that you need your children, Sergeant, and now that I am old both of my children are gone, dead and buried."

"I knew about your daughter," said Milton. "I didn't know you had a son."

"It was in the War; he was killed at Salerno. He's buried there."

"I'm sorry."

"That was why Selina called her son Tom, Thomas Derek. Her husband tried to persuade her against it."

"Do you know where her husband is now?"

"In Cape Town."

"Do you have his address?"

"No."

"Would you know if he corresponds with his son?"

"He does not."

"Are you sure?"

"I am certain."

Milton looked at his notebook. "I understand his name is George Howard Brockhouse."

"Yes, you'll find him easily enough if you want to. He's a design engineer; he'll be well known in the best clubs of Cape Town, whatever they are. Or any of the barmen in the big hotels."

"He may"—Milton paused slightly—"it's possible that he has remarried and has another family."

"He is certainly married; he remarried in 1952."

"1952?"

"Three months after my daughter's death he married a girl eighteen years younger than himself, a girl who had caused my daughter—some unhappiness."

"Would your grandson have known this?"

156

"He knew his father had married again."

"I see."

"Perhaps you do see : it can't be an uncommon situation. Young Tom never asked about his father, he said he could hardly remember him."

"Did his father ever write to him?"

"There were cards for the first few years, birthday money-orders, that sort of thing : rarely in his father's handwriting. I adopted him legally when he was fourteen years old."

"Was he a happy boy?"

"I believe so. He was always quiet and well behaved, rather more solitary than I would have liked. He enjoyed the country, but he was too dreamy for a farmer. He was nothing like my son. He was very fond of shooting. He took over my vermin gun when he was very small. He was a natural shot."

In the little silence that followed the old man turned his calm eyes back to the snapshot of his grandson. Small comforting sounds filled the shed; starlings called to each other from the roof of the house, the chair of the old man creaked, and from far across the fields came the lowing of cows at pasture. Some insect caught in the upper part of the shed sawed angrily in the rafters.

"Tom was always a bright boy, both in the local school here when he was small and at his grammar school. He learnt things very quickly, and he was very well thought of by his teachers. He was an ingratiating boy : he had the gift of sensing what would please other people and then showing them that side of his character which he knew would appeal to them. In that he was similar to his father, who was always— very plausible."

"Did you know he took drugs?"

"No."

"You don't appear to be very surprised."

"I've had a feeling that something was wrong. I didn't know what, but I've had this feeling for some time that things were not right."

"When did you first feel that?"

"It arose gradually. I suppose I first became aware of it three years ago."

"When he was at university?"

"He changed when he went to London. He seemed to have little to talk about when he came up here on holiday, in his vacations. He had no interest. As time went on he came less frequently."

"What did he do when he was here?"

"He spent most of his time in his room, reading—curious books, some of them. When he went out it was to go shooting, always alone. My wife tried very hard to encourage him to meet people more, to go to the young farmers' dances and that sort of thing."

"When was he last here?"

"Five weeks ago. He arrived ten days before that. He looked very tired and said that he had a lot of studying to do for an examination. The day after he arrived he spent mostly in bed; he said he was very tired, and he ate hardly anything. He wouldn't let me call a doctor, and was a lot better the day after. He said that he had been to a doctor in London, who had told him that he had been studying for too long a period at once, but that he would be all right if he rested for a day if he felt exhausted."

"Did you believe him?"

"No, I didn't wholly believe him."

"Did he receive any letters or have any visitors while he was here?"

"Neither."

"Solitary, you said, as a boy."

The old man got up from his chair and took a large flower-pot down from one of the shelves on the end wall. From within it he took out a cardboard box which he carried back to his chair. Milton watched in silence as he resumed his seat.

"After he had left I went up to his room. It is something I have never done before: he has always been able to return and find his things exactly as he had left them. I wanted to know if he had taken his shotgun."

"And had he?"

"No, it was dismantled and inside a suitcase in his wardrobe. It was one of the suitcases he had with him when he first arrived. Besides the shotgun there were also these."

The old man put the cardboard box on the rustic table and took out its contents one by one. First he took out two long, very thin knives each wrapped up in a piece of oily rag, then a handful of 9 mm. nickel-headed bullets, a box of shotgun cartridges, and a large Perspex tube of tablets: it had no label, and the tablets were blue. Finally the old man placed a Manila envelope on the table.

Milton picked up one of the 9 mm. bullets. "Does he have any other gun?"

The old man sighed. "His father brought one home as a souvenir from the War. He was in the infantry in Italy."

"Do you remember what it was?"

"It was a Luger pistol. It was kept up in the attic for years with all his other trophies: a steel helmet, ceremonial dagger, death's-head cap, things like that. George used to talk about having a den and putting them up on the walls."

"Where is the pistol now?"

"It's gone."

"Did you ever suspect that your grandson could have been involved in a serious crime? In the shooting of Constable Toms?"

"It never crossed my mind until yesterday." The old man picked up the Manila envelope and slid from it a wad of newspaper cuttings; they were reports of the shooting of Toms. As Milton glanced at them the old man upended the envelope and shook out a number of photographs; Milton could see at a glance that they were indecent. They were all black-and-white photographs of postcard size. One of them Milton examined closely: the girl involved was Elizabeth Jenkins.

"I'll have to take these with me."

"I understand that."

"And the shotgun."

"I'll get it for you when we go into the house."

Milton began to collect up the items from the table. The old man put them back into the cardboard box for him.

"There's one other thing I would like to ask you," said Milton. "You've obviously used shotguns a lot yourself. Have you ever heard of anyone removing the shot from a cartridge?"

The old man remained very still, his chin jutting forward over the hands clasped on his stick. His eyes were unblinking. An underlying emotion arose in the atmosphere which made Milton feel slightly uneasy and want to clear his throat.

"Ten years ago," said the old man eventually, "a shooting-party was made up to clear off pests from some of the adjoining land. One of the local lads, who fancied himself as a marks-man, unknown to him, had his gun loaded with shotless cart-ridges. It was a joke."

"Yes," said Milton.

For the first time the old man did not meet his eye. "The lad fired his first barrel at close range, and, of course, his target flew off. He guessed what had happened. He had a quick temper, and when he saw the others laughing at him he was furious. He threw the gun wide, and the second barrel fired. He blinded his younger brother." Milton felt his lumbar muscles harden, and the hairs along his spine and neck rise up.

"Your grandson knew?"

The old voice was thick. "He saw it happen."

Milton looked away from the old man, to the snapshot of the young boy. When he looked back the old eyes had grown calm again.

"Have you any idea where your grandson could be now?"

"You don't know?"

"We'll find him eventually. It would be better for everyone if we could find him soon."

The old man said nothing.

"I can appreciate how you feel towards your grandson, Mr Mitchell, but a policeman has been blinded. Anybody who could do that deliberately could do anything. We have to find your grandson, for his own sake, among other things. He may have certain reasons, he may need some sort of treatment: a court will listen to reasons."

"And when you find him what will you do?"

"Arrest him."

160

"He has blinded a policeman."

"Yes."

"And if he resists arrest?"

"Well. . . ."

"It's likely, isn't it, that he will be the worse for wear because he resisted arrest?"

"If he resists we're bound to defend ourselves. If he comes quietly he'll be all right. We wouldn't set about him for the sake of it."

The old man looked Milton full in the face. His eyes were very calm and very clear.

"I would," he said, "if it was one of mine."

He put his hand inside his jacket and drew out a piece of paper. He put this into Milton's hand and stood up. He left the hut, and through the open door Milton saw him walk across the yard to the house. He was very erect.

Milton looked down at the paper. It was a letter, very brief and to the point, in neatly formed handwriting.

I will be staying here for some time. It is much better than my old room. There is far more privacy and I don't have to look at so many other people's chimneys. There is a park quite near, not that I see much of it. I really am getting down to my books now.

It was signed 'Tom', and the address was 17 Courthope Terrace, W.12.

Milton got up and walked slowly after the old man.

25

MILTON got back in to London shortly after eleven o'clock. He had had to rise at the crack of dawn in order to catch the only train that would get him back before midday, but Davies had been most insistent. He had slept badly in the commercial hotel that Wilson had found for him, but that had been mainly due to the fact that after reporting to Davies he had spent the rest of the evening in matching pints of the local beer with Inspector Gearing of the Shrewsbury C.I.D.

When he got back to the station the desk day sergeant told him that Davies was waiting for him, and had given orders that he was to go straight up before doing anything else. Davies was in his usual stance at his desk, elbows planted on either side of his blotting-pad, chin propped up on his knuckles, and the pipe hanging loosely down like the pendulum of a broken clock. He nodded to Milton, and watched him lift the parcels up on to his desk and unwrap them. Milton laid the shotgun carefully across the blotting-pad and arranged the contents of the cardboard box around it before he sat down in the chair opposite the desk, rather irked by Davies's silence.

Davies stared moodily down for some time before he finally broke his pose to run a reflective finger along the barrel of the shotgun. "So this is it."

Milton nodded. "Luck, really. The old man was brooding about it, and ready to unload when I arrived. Any other time there wouldn't have been anything."

Davies nodded. "You did well, a lot better than I thought

you would, I'll admit that." He removed his pipe and passed a weary hand across his eyes. "On any other case it would be enough, more than enough."

"He might break."

Davies grinned savagely. "I've spent the best part of three hours with him, up to about ten minutes before you got here."

"Brockhouse?"

"We brought him in at nine o'clock this morning. The house has been watched since you phoned in last night and I gave orders to bring him in if he tried to leave it, and that's what he did at nine. He didn't have this Luger his grandfather says he took. He had nothing, drugs, guns, knives, or dirty photographs. I've had him examined by a doctor, and there are no marks on him—syringes, I mean. If he does take drugs then they're soft ones, pep pills, that sort of thing. We searched his room, and everything in it is over there on the table. We went through the rest of the house and found nothing. His landlady thinks that the sun shines out of his arse. He had about thirty books in his room : it's about all there was there, and not one of them's by the Marquis de Sade."

"What sort of books are they?"

"Help yourself." Davies waved him towards the side table.

Milton picked up half a dozen or so of the books and stood them up between his hands so that he could read the titles. *A Dictionary of Philosophy; Principia Mathematica; Da Vinci Sketchbooks; Race, Prejudice and Education; Waste Makers; Motivations of Commerce; Psychology of the Crowd; Principles of Logic.*

"Intelligent bastard, isn't he?" said Davies.

"I can't see these connecting up with any university course."

"So what, Arthur?—it's not a crime not to go to college or to allow your grandfather to believe that you are. Those books don't help us at all. I've had him for nigh on three hours, and I tried everything I know and got nothing. He's been reading the laws of evidence, and he knows that all he has to do is to sit there and say nothing and we've got to prove every damn thing we say he did."

"He says nothing?"

"All he mentions is the time, points out how long he's been here. I've told him about his grandfather, told him we've got the shotgun, everything you said on the phone. He just doesn't answer. It's unnatural. I've met clever criminals before, shrewd, cunning bastards, but I've never met one like this. It's a funny thing talking to him, Arthur; he didn't say a word, but I'm now convinced he did Toms, did him with this gun. He's the joker that girl was talking about all right, no doubt about it. How old is he, twenty-two. That means he's just starting, so Christ knows what he's going to be like if he's not stopped."

"We could charge him on these." Milton picked up the tube of amphetamine tablets from the desk.

"We could, but possession's a bit tricky. He didn't have them on him, did he? They were found in Shropshire. It would have to be done up there. No, Arthur, let him think he's made a fool of us, see where he runs to. He's got that Luger somewhere."

"He'll know he's being watched."

"I know, and being as bright as he is he's not likely to give us a chance, but what else can we do while we put our story together? All we can do now is to turn what we've got over to the D.P.P. and see if we've got a case."

"I think it's pretty impressive."

"Things always sound different in court when the lawyers have had a go at them. The trouble with what we've got is that it's circumstantial—nothing's backed up. You can't beat a good solid piece of evidence that you can hang everything else on to—a fingerprint, ballistics, mud-traces, or a good honest eye-witness, someone a jury can identify with."

"Where's Brockhouse now?"

"In the interview-room with a constable. I thought he could stew a bit."

"I'd like to see him."

"Why not? Show him this." He lifted the gun up from his desk. "You never know your luck; but we can't keep him much longer, not if he insists like he has been. When you've had your chat let him go. I'll have a man waiting for him."

"Right." Milton picked up the shotgun and went down the

corridor to the interview-room. He tapped on the door. It was opened by a uniformed constable who shook his head slightly to indicate that the suspect had said nothing to him. Milton waited until the constable had left and closed the door behind him before he turned towards the boy sitting on the other side of the interview table. He had finely balanced features, his skin was without blemish, and his eyes were a cool, untroubled grey. His hair, brushed boyishly across his forehead, was very pale, the colour that on a girl would have been called ash-blonde. His mouth, chin, and eyes were very evenly and neatly proportioned. He wore a high-necked black cashmere sweater, and a dark suede jacket with light-blue casual trousers. He sat on the hard-backed interview-room chair, showing no signs of discomfort. He looked slightly bored.

Milton sat down on the other side of the interview table, carefully laying the shotgun across its length, so that it was between them. Then he put both elbows on the table and studied the boy, who looked back with indifference.

"Your name is Thomas Derek Brockhouse, is that right?"

"Who are you?"

"Detective Sergeant Milton."

The boy examined Milton's face very coolly before he shifted his gaze down to the cuff of his right wrist, pulled back the sleeve of his suede jacket, and bared the dial of a large gold wrist-watch. "Yes, Detective Sergeant Milton, I am Thomas Derek Brockhouse. I have now been here for three hours and twenty-five minutes, and I wish either to be allowed to contact my solicitor or to know the details of any charge that is being made against me."

"Been messing you about, have they, lad—asking a lot of silly questions?"

The boy looked at him with something very like contempt, glanced down at the shotgun, and sighed.

"You have to make allowances, lad. Not all of us are up to talking with a bright lad like you. I don't pretend to be myself; very little education I've had, hardly ever read a book, but it takes all sorts after all. No, I came to talk about the gun. Don't be frightened to look at it, no harm in owning a shotgun, especially up in your home country. Nice up there, it is. Go on, lad, pick it up, we know it's yours; must be a few days since you've handled it. How long since you've done any shooting?"

The boy's eyelids closed like shutters, and when they opened again his eyes were completely blank. "I've now been here for three and a half hours, and I am still awaiting details of a charge or an opportunity to telephone my solicitor."

"Your grandfather is a fine old man. It's been a long time since I've met anyone with as much character, you can see it in his face, it's all there—"

"I've now been here—"

"Now your face: that's an interesting face. I suppose you know a bit about them yourself, studied them. You would, a bright boy like you. And you're a bit of an actor, aren't you, lad—put on the face you think people would like to see—but, of course, I'm a professional. Not bright or anything like that, but experienced. I see a lot of faces, been looking at them for years and learning a bit about them—almost in spite of myself, as you might say. Angry faces, frightened faces, all sorts. I know the face of innocence, for example. It isn't yours. Innocence isn't unconcern, not in a police station it isn't: it's bewilderment, confusion, it's out of its depth, you see; bit pathetic, innocence is. You'd never stand for being pathetic, would you, lad?"

"I've been here for three hours and forty minutes. . . ."

"Nothing like a talking clock at all. Now calculation is something else, you can always tell when someone's been calculating, reading up the laws of evidence, for example, like a shark lawyer. An innocent man would never do that, probably have no idea what laws of evidence are. You get what I'm talking about, don't you, lad? A clever chap like you would get my point right away."

Brockhouse looked at him straight in the eye but said nothing.

"And not being innocent you wouldn't want to answer?"

The boy scraped back his chair and stood up abruptly. Milton did not move. "As I've been here for over three and a half hours," said Brockhouse, "and no-one has told me of any charge, I assume I have not been arrested. I was asked to come here to assist inquiries; having done so, I am going home." He pulled the zip of the suede jacket, closing the ends up to the throat and raising up the collar so that it stood up around his neck. "Unless there is a charge."

"No," said Milton, "no charge. How could we have any evidence for a charge?"

"Why was I brought here, then?"

"We wanted to meet you, talk to you, see what you looked like. We get curious too. We wanted to see what kind of a human being you are, and now, of course, we know."

The boy held Milton's glance, reluctant to lower his eyes, but eventually he turned away and pulled back the door of the interview-room. He went out, leaving it open. Milton did not immediately follow him; he remained at the table in an imitation of Davies's favourite pose, elbows on the table, chin in hands. He continued staring at the chair opposite in which the boy had sat for some time, then he sighed and began searching his pockets for a cigarette to take away the touch of nausea he had at the back of his throat.

26

THE file on Brockhouse, together with the report on which Davies had sweated blood for three days, was sent to the department of the Director of Public Prosecutions. It was more than a week before anything was heard from that august institution. Brockhouse remained under twenty-four-hour surveillance, and it was playing hell with the duty rosters. Milton grew progressively morose; he plunged into more and more of the bread-and-butter cases, working five or six hours overtime each night. His constables tried to avoid him, and only Newcombe still visited the C.I.D. room socially. Milton's irritability intensified in inverse ratio to the lack of information in the reports of Brockhouse's watchers. He led a solitary existence; left his room between nine and ten o'clock and had breakfast in the café at the corner of the road in which he lodged. If it was fine he walked to Ealing Common or Gunnersbury Park, more occasionally to Kew Gardens. He then either strolled about (causing great difficulties to the men who were watching him) or sat on a bench reading a book he had brought with him. If it was raining he went to the public library and sat in the reference section. He lunched at one of two resturants, both close to Acton Town station, and each offering a set meal for five shillings.

As he went to eat lunch at around one o'clock the restaurants were usually crowded. Brockhouse would take any odd seat at an already occupied table. The large number of other customers made surveillance difficult, but Brockhouse did not appear to speak to anyone. On two occasions he had joined the table of three young men with whom he had sat before, but this did not appear to be significant. In the afternoons he sometimes went to the library if he had not already been there in the morning, but more usually he entered one of the local cinemas. He did not seem to care which picture was showing; one afternoon he had spent in a betting-shop. At about six o'clock he returned to his room and stayed there until morning. The hall telephone at his lodgings was monitored, but Brockhouse had neither made nor received any calls. He had not used a public telephone. He had not posted or received any letters. None of his watchers had seen him speak to anyone during his walks, in the library, the café, restaurants, or cinemas. Brockhouse had made no sign that he knew he was under surveillance.

He was always dressed in his blue casual trousers, black sweater, and suede jacket. He carried the books he read in a plastic document case. The case appeared empty while he was reading his book; there was no bulge in the jacket. He was almost certainly not carrying a Luger automatic pistol.

Two weeks after the file went to the Director of Public Prosecutions Davies was asked to call upon the Deputy Director. His appointment was for eleven o'clock, and Milton waited for him in the saloon bar of a public house called the Wheatsheaf. He sat gloomily drinking glass after glass of light ale, which steadily built up a gaseous bulge in his abused stomach and brought on his heartburn. He watched the bar fill up from twelve o'clock onward with chief clerks and office managers who preferred not to lunch with their staffs. Hardly any of them sat at the tables : they stood in a pack at the bar, chewing beef sandwiches and drinking halves of bitter. Every two minutes or so they went into convulsions over a dirty story of which Milton could hear nothing except an occasional punch-line.

Davies arrived shortly after one o'clock. He came in slowly and deliberately and in a filthy temper. He scowled at the crowded bar and nodded curtly to Milton. He snapped his fingers imperiously over the head of a thin man with spectacles, and was served at once. He carried a pint of bitter and a large whisky over to Milton's table. He shoved the pint at Milton carelessly, spilling some of the beer so that it ran up Milton's sleeve.

Davies spread himself into the corner seat, his girth filling out the whole of one side, the glass of whisky hidden within his huge fist. Milton looked inquiringly at him, but got nothing in return except a ferocious scowl directed somewhere to the side of his left ear. Milton picked up his pint of bitter, and had drunk about two-thirds of it before anything was said.

"They say we haven't got a case." Davies swallowed his whisky in a single gulp and banged the glass down on the little table. A small man at the bar in a trilby hat looked round, caught Davies's eye, and turned hurriedly back again.

"It stands up to me."

"It doesn't, they're bloody right it doesn't, too bloody right. It's the old story; we've been too close to it. I've just been through it with them as it would come out in court. Don't forget that this crap-hound hasn't got any form to start with, and whatever mouthpiece he gets hold of will make a meal of that. He's a baby-faced student with a spotless reputation who lost his mother when he was eight, so you'll have the jury ready to give him a pound out of the poor-box for a start. What evidence have we got? Poor old Toms can't identify him. The only man who ever saw him in Legume Street was Lloyd, and he only saw his back and thought his hair was white."

"The car?"

"What about it? The only link between him and the car is Carter, and he'd get crucified in the box. No judge would let Carter's evidence in without corroboration."

"And it doesn't tie Brockhouse with the car on that night, it was five days after. Carter wouldn't go into the box anyway."

"Right, so the only real witness we've got is the girl and she's a slag, she looks like a slag. She's got a record, and she's a drug-addict; some witness."

"Come to think about it, he's dumped her anyway—they could show malice."

"That's what I meant about being too close. So what else?

170

We've got the bullets from outside the cemetery, but we've got to match them up with the gun. That'll take some doing. Even if we got ballistic evidence, we'd have to prove he had the gun at that time, and I bet he's got rid of it. We can't put the old man in the box, or that prosy bastard you saw. . . ."

"Grimaldi?"

"Grimaldi. He makes sense about Brockhouse, but what he says would sound like a lot of cock to most people. Pawson can't identify him from the cemetery. A jury might swing against him for using his mother's grave for holding drugs if you had got him in the cemetery. But even if that hadn't been a balls-up we could only have had him for possession of drugs and the gun."

"It would have been better than nothing. If we'd had that to hold him on we could have worked on him, built it up."

"I wouldn't bet on it. He's a clever sod, let's face it."

"So he just walks away."

"Until the next time." Davies twisted the stem of his pipe violently in its seating. "There's always a next time. With this joker there's sure to be."

"I'm not so sure."

"I am; I don't believe in supermen."

"Nor do I."

"No-one expects you to like it, Arthur. You try to do your job, it's the same job as I try to do. Neither of us make the laws, we enforce them, and if the six hundred soft-boiled eggs up in Westminster make us enforce them with one hand tied behind our backs, then they can't complain if blokes like Brockhouse are left to run loose."

"We could—"

"I don't want to hear about it."

"I—"

"It's over; it finished when the lawyers turned it down. Brockhouse will be on file, he won't always be lucky."

"And if he comes back under another name?"

Davies shrugged, struck a match, and watched it burn almost away before he applied it to the bowl of his pipe. "Look, Arthur, I know how you feel, and I know why you feel it on this particular case. There's always one that we take personally. But remember what you are; you are a policeman, you're not a judge, a jury, or an executioner." Davies got up. "Stop thinking about it, you can't set the world right on your own, and if you try you'll go mad."

"He blinds Toms, cripples Pawson, does God knows what else, and get's away with it. He's laughing at us."

"Keep your voice down." Davies looked down at him rather sadly. "I've seen it happen before, good men being eaten away. If you can't take a man within the law you've got to grit your teeth and wear it. You can't afford to take any of it personally. If you do you move outside the law and become a criminal yourself." He turned towards the door. "Don't do anything silly, Arthur."

Milton watched him go out of the door and continued to stare after him for some time before he got up and went to the bar to buy himself another drink.

27

THAT evening Milton was still in a pub, but this time it was the Feathers round the corner to the station. He was waiting for Newcombe; he had been there for an hour, sitting in the corner next to the window, and since he had sat there he had downed five double whiskies. Apart from flushing his cheeks and neck, they had not affected him. He was coldly sober.

While he had been waiting he had been making a number of calculations at the back of his notebook. Milton rarely troubled to think much about the sort of money he was paid : he took it as it came, and whatever passed through his hands never lasted long. Now that it was necessary to know what it all amounted to he was finding that it required some thought. As a first-class sergeant with London allowance, and detective duty pay on top, his basic salary came to the rather curious sum of £1,401 per year. On top of that he worked a lot of over-time : he had to wrestle with that for some time before he decided that it came to about another £200. That made it nearly £31 a week. He wrote it down below his jottings, and drew a circle.

A shout came from the door and he looked up to see that Newcombe, in thrusting the door brutally open, had thumped it into the behind of a tidy-looking man who had at that moment been in the act of bending forward to set some drinks down on one of the little tables. The man shot upright, and held his soaking cuffs towards Newcombe, who did not seem to see them. He made straight for the bar, where the landlord was already drawing up his pint of bitter. Newcombe drank more than half of it in one long draught before he turned away from the bar and sat himself on the chair opposite Milton. He was wearing his old raincoat. It was too small for him to button across his chest, and he allowed it to hang carelessly open to show his uniform.

"Well," he said.

"Well, Henry." Milton glanced down at his notebook. "I've been trying to see how much I need to live on."

"How much is it?"

"I've worked it out that I get about thirty pounds now."

"You've forgotten your rent allowance; every bleeder takes it for granted. You'd soon notice if you didn't have it. So you need thirty-six pounds a week to live on, and who do you think is going to pay that out to a beaten-up old bastard like you?"

"What would you do if you left the Force now, Henry?"

"Keep a pub." He belched loudly.

"I wouldn't be any good at that."

"No, you wouldn't, you've got the face of an undertaker; you'd remind all the poor bastards of what they'd come into a boozer to forget."

"Thanks."

"Well, stop horsing around," said Newcombe, "what's it all about?"

"They say we haven't got a case."

"I know."

"I'm going to have him, Henry, I'm going to have Mr Thomas Brockhouse, and since I can't do it as a copper I'm jacking it in."

"You're off your bleeding nut." Newcombe crashed down his fist, making his pint mug leap six inches up from the table.

"Keep your bloody voice down."

Newcombe looked long and hard at Milton. "What are you going to do, wait for him up an alley?"

"I'll think of something."

"You're bloody pathetic," said Newcombe. "What are you going to hit him with, a half-brick?" He spat a broken piece of matchstick from between his teeth.

"I'm not letting go. I'm not doing nothing. This is one bastard who is going to get what's coming to him, or I'll go down trying."

"Why stop at Brockhouse? Why not get on your white horse about Griffen? He knocks people over every other day. He's put two in mental hospitals through banging their brains about already this year, or is it different because he uses his boys to do it?"

"I don't care who Griffen puts down, they're a load of rubbish anyway. They'd be doing the same to him if things were turned round the other way. All Griffen does, when you come right down to it, is what we ought to do but can't—keep the weeds down. Listen, Henry, Toms wasn't blinded because of an unlucky shot, this bastard went out of his way to blind him, and he got the idea for it when he saw it happen to a kid by accident. He's special all right."

Newcombe slowly shook his huge head. "I wonder what the hell you've been up to for the last twenty years. I'd have thought some of it would have rubbed off. You've got no idea of how to go about it. All you've got is this Simon Pure idea of not soiling your lily-white copper's hands, and you think that you'll suddenly be different once you've turned it in. You berk!"

"You're wasting your breath, Henry. I want him."

"And you think you're the only one?"

"Who else?"

"Me."

"And what are you going to do about it?"

"What I'm not going to do is walk about with some half-arsed idea of playing Robin Hood." Newcombe rummaged around inside one of his breast pockets and brought out a dirty piece of paper. "Where do Griffen's layabouts hang out at night?"

"I'm not having any truck with that rubbish."

"Who said you were—or me?" Newcombe barked out what

passed with him as a laugh. "Get some wallop in and I'll tell you what's going to happen to Brockhouse."

Milton picked up the piece of paper. "What's at 75 Glendale Drive?"

"Get the beer in."

28

NEWCOMBE double-parked his old Austin alongside a derelict Buick and a motor-cycle combination standing in the road outside 75 Glendale Drive. It was a gloomy Victorian villa with three stone steps leading up to the front door; all three were broken. The front garden was a patch of straggling grass, littered with old tin cans, pieces of bicycles, half-bricks, and broken prams. On the door was a long line of bell-pushes and a list of hand-written cards; Newcombe struck a match, he struck several before he found Pinky's card— "Mr Price, Flat 9". He put his finger on the bell-push and held it there. Nothing happened. He thumped the door with his fist, and still nothing happened : he pressed all the bell-pushes in turn and stood back to apply his size twelve to the door until the old brown paint flaked down in a small storm.

From above came a number of angry shouts, faces appeared at windows, and somewhere on the ground floor a baby started crying. At long last an unsteady shuffling sounded from behind the door, a thin voice shouted, but Newcombe continued kicking the door. Finally the bolt was drawn and the door slightly opened; the face that looked out was unrecognizably distorted with sleep and rage.

"What the soddin' 'ell's up?"

Newcombe hit the door with the whole of his weight, and the man behind it went flying. There was the hell of a crash as he cannoned backward into a heaped-up pram and turned it upside down into a heap at the foot of the stairs. The man came forward in a crouch. He was short but very broad, wisps of hair stuck up from his balding head. His trousers were slipping over his hips. Newcombe opened his raincoat to show his uniform.

"Where's Price?"

The man hesitated. "Stay out of it," said Newcombe. "Where's Price?"

"Get stuffed."

Newcombe went past him and up the stairs, not troubling to step over the things from the pram that were strewn over the lower steps. The staircase was mostly the original wood with only scraps of linoleum, so worn that they had shredded and wedded themselves to the stair-treads. The only other thing on the stairs was a smell of stale cabbage. Newcombe went up, beyond the first landing, which was cluttered with prams and bicycles; the doors were marked 4 to 8. He went up the next stairs, and on top of that was another landing with two unmarked doors. The roof came down at a pitched angle; these were the attic rooms. On one of the doors was a crudely chalked "10". Newcombe pushed the other door. There was no lock on it, it was held shut by a chair that scraped aside as soon as Newcombe put pressure on the door.

Pinky's room was depressing: there were large damp-stains on the walls, and the ceiling radiated cracks from the light-flex. The floor was covered with worn-out linoleum, the windows were filthy, and one of the panes had been replaced by a piece of unpainted hardboard. Apart from the iron-framed bed, heaped with Army blankets, there were only two wooden chairs; one by the bed heaped with Pinky's worldly possessions. His coat and shirt hung from a six-inch nail hammered into one of the cracks in the plaster. It was hardly bigger than a prison cell, and the smell was worse. The whole room stank of dirt and bad personal habits: of unwashed socks, grimy feet, stale beer, blocked drains, and sour food.

Newcombe tried not to breathe too deeply. He crashed his right boot viciously against the foot of the bed. Pinky shot up from the heap of blankets like a startled rabbit, his thin hair standing up on end and his mouth gaping toothlessly. He peered at Newcombe with red-rimmed, beady eyes, and from under the blankets he brought out a ten-inch hunting-knife.

"Get up, Pinky."

"For Christ's sake."

"Put your knife away," said Newcombe, "before I have you for possession of an offensive weapon."

"Mr Newcombe! For Christ's sake, what's up?"

"Get dressed, and be bloody quick about it."

Pinky scrambled out from under the blankets in his torn singlet and underpants. He was already wearing his socks, but he still swore violently as his feet hit the coldness of the bare floor. He shot Newcombe a look of blinding hatred as he fumbled for his trousers: underneath them, on the chair, were his false teeth, and he snatched them into his mouth. Newcombe felt a slight nausea. Pinky sat down again on the edge of the bed to put on his shoes. On the floor beside it was a saucer full of dog-ends. Pinky sorted one out and put it in his mouth: he struck a match with a shaking hand and drew in a lungful of smoke. Newcombe waited until he had finished coughing.

"It's about this pretty boy."

"You shouldn't have come here, Mr Newcombe, you really shouldn't have come."

"Get stuffed."

"It's not right. I've never done you any harm, and I'm an old man."

"Oh, for Christ's sake stop whining. It'll look all right, I'll take you out of here with my hand on your collar."

"Take me in? What the bleedin' 'ell for?"

"What's the going price for Brockhouse?"

"Who?"

"What's Griffen paying?"

"What d'you mean?"

"Stop sodding about, Pinky, or I really will take you in. Griffen wants him, he can't find him. How much is he paying?"

Incredulity passed across Pinky's face. "You want to sell him?"

"I'm selling nothing. Is the price still out for him or not?"

"It's out, half a ton for anyone who sees him, and you know what that means: you might be lucky to see ten or even five. But he can't be in the Smoke, can he? He'd be seen by now."

"Depends on what you mean by London," said Newcombe. He lit a cigarette in self-defence against the room.

"But you want him, don't you, leastways your boss does, for Toms?"

"Who says so?"

Pinky looked bewildered. He sucked his cigarette end thoughtfully, and then his face twisted up in an unlovely smile. "I get it, you can't hang it on him, eh, Mr Newcombe?"

"Shut your face."

"All right, all right," said Pinky, intimidated for one rare moment in his life. He looked up at Newcombe's towering bulk and scratched himself. "What do you want me to do?"

"Get your coat on," said Newcombe.

They went down the stairs. Newcombe was even more careless of the amount of noise he created, and most of the doors opened stealthily as they passed. Newcombe, gripping Pinky's arm, shoved him down the stairs in front of him. He could hear the muttered "Bastard" clearly as he passed each landing.

Down in the hall the balding man had disappeared. Pinky opened the front door and they went down the stone steps. Newcombe still held on to Pinky's arm as they went through the front gate. He did not trouble to look back to the house to watch the enraged faces at the windows, but Pinky did. "They reckon I've had it," he said gleefully. "I'll tell 'em when I go back that you 'ad to apologize."

"Tell them what the hell you like."

Newcombe put the car into gear. "Where's the nearest phone box?"

"Up round the corner. I'll get through to Griffen 'imself, tell him I see Brockhouse while I was visiting a mate, how about that?"

"17 Courthope Terrace; it's off Wood Lane."

"Shepherd's Bush, eh. He's a chancer, he could easy be seen there."

180

"Well, he was, wasn't he?" said Newcombe. He threw the car into the kerb at the telephone kiosk.

"See if the phone's O.K."

"Righto!"

Pinky scuttled across the pavement and Newcombe extracted from the back of his notebook a much-folded and worn five-pound note. Pinky scuttled back.

"All O.K., Mr Newcombe, I've got me sixpence." He stared in wonder at the fiver. "That ain't necessary, ain't necessary at all, I don't want no money from you."

Newcombe shoved the fiver into the front of Pinky's shirt. "I always pay for what I want, then I don't owe any favours." He let the clutch up savagely, jerking Pinky away from the window. As he accelerated up the middle of the road he could see in his rear-view mirror that Pinky was still on the edge of the pavement looking after him in bewilderment. Then he was at the corner, and as he changed down he looked again in the mirror and saw that Pinky was going into the telephone kiosk.

He accelerated out of the corner and kept a sharp look-out for another telephone box. At the very end of the road, set back by some shops, was a police box. He drove across to the wrong side of the road and jumped out, leaving the door swinging over the pavement.

29

SHORTLY before midnight on Thursday, March 17th, Mr Gordon Andrews, a dispatch clerk living in West Ealing, made an excited emergency call from a public telephone box. He reported that while walking with his dog along the Goldhawk Road he had seen a young man with fair hair attacked by two men who jumped from a large black car that had pulled suddenly across from the other side of the road. The young man had tried to run from the men, but had been felled by a blow from the larger of his two assailants. He had then been bundled into the back of the car, which had been driven off at high speed towards Park Royal. The car was dark-coloured and Mr Andrews thought that it resembled a Jaguar, but he could not be sure; the number-plate was indistinguishable. Mr Andrews could not say whether anyone else was in the car. He did not have a clear view of the assailants or of the victim. The attack had taken place twenty minutes before he was able to find a call-box that was in working order.

30

MILTON hunched himself inside a huge greatcoat of blue melton that was half an inch thick. He had borrowed it from the sergeant in charge of the Port of London floating police station. His face ached from the bitingly cold wind coming off the river. The ends of his fingers were numb, and his eyes watered, but for the first time in weeks his head was clear.

Shortly before four o'clock that morning a body had been taken from the water at Wapping Old Stairs. It was the body of a young man with fair hair, five feet nine inches in height, and about twenty years of age. The body was clothed in trousers and shirt, both heavily soiled; there was no jacket, no tie, and no shoes. There were no papers or anything else in the pockets which could be used for identification, but on the inside of the leather belt holding up the trousers there was written, in indelible pencil, the word "Brockhouse".

Davies, as the officer originating the request for information on Brockhouse, received the call at his home, and he rather maliciously ordered Milton to follow it up. Milton had no doubt that Davies had turned his square bulk over in bed as soon as he had put down the receiver. Milton had been interviewing the driver of a stolen lorry when the call had come through, and he had been looking forward to finishing his shift of duty. He had handed the lorry driver over to Detective Constable Perkins, the young replacement for George Pawson.

Now here he was, by one gauge of time three months and seventeen days after Toms had walked up to a car in Legume Street: and by another half a lifetime ago.

It was all over. The man about whose throat he had closed his hands a thousand times in his imagination was now lying broken on the wet planking at his feet, and all he could feel was a strange pity at his frailty. The station sergeant had pulled away the blanket covering the body, and for the fragment of a second the ridiculous protest crossed Milton's mind that it was inhuman to leave anyone exposed on such a bitter morning.

The station sergeant was a grizzled man with thick bushy eyebrows whose main concern appeared to be the rolling of a perfectly cylindrical and very thin shag cigarette. He licked the gummed edge of the cigarette paper and glanced down indifferently.

"It makes a change," he said, "from the birds we fish out. Young birds or old men. You don't get blokes his age knocking themselves off very often."

Milton crouched down to peer closely at Brockhouse's face: the eyes were open, and despite their being caked with mud it was possible to detect a look within them of guarded acceptance. Either to detect or imagine such a look.

"See that on the side of his face," said the sergeant, "looks like a lump of mud? It's a bruise. He must have gone the hell of a thump. Hit a bridge stanchion or something as he went in."

"Very likely," said Milton.

"If he'd been thumped by a barge or a log it wouldn't come up like that, not once he was dead." The sergeant bared very discoloured teeth. He seemed to be enjoying himself. "Seems stupid, don't it, not being allowed to move him till a sawbones says he's dead?" He moved one of the bare feet with his boot. "Not much doubt about him, is there?"

"Would he have been in there long?"

"Can't tell, not within a day, even the pathologists. He won't have been in all that long, though, it's not blown up with gas,

184

but that would be slowed down a bit by the cold. It's been cold lately."

"I know."

"Been a right bastard down here." He scraped his boot along the planking. "He won't have been long; three, four days. Is it important?"

"It would help."

"What do you want him for?"

"Nothing now."

The station sergeant snorted and then spat past Milton into the water. "It's not a State secret," said Milton. "He could have cleared up a case for us."

"Murder?"

"Malicious wounding."

"They make too much of a do about murder—the papers, I mean. It's only G.B.H. gone over the top. Ah, here he comes, the ornament of the medical profession!"

Down the cakewalk came a tall young man with unruly hair. He wore a herringbone overcoat with the collar turned up. His face was very pale in the cold brilliant light reflected back from the water.

"Here he is, Doctor."

The doctor nodded to the sergeant and bent over the body without speaking. He touched the body, and almost immediately rose again. "I'll send the certificate."

"Bit nippy this morning, Doctor. Like a mug of tea?"

"Not just now, Sergeant, I want to get back to the surgery." He nodded to Milton and turned back to the cakewalk. They watched his return, the station sergeant with particular interest. As the doctor flinched at a sudden squall the sergeant chuckled. "Get back to the surgery, my arse, he's off to the nest. The other one, the senior partner, you can't raise him, not for these jobs. That one's Derek, a nice feller, he's only got married two months ago, and a fair old piece of crumpet she is. Not fair, really, to pull a bloke out of a bed like that to come and look at this, is it?"

"What happens now?"

185

"Burke and Hare. The coffin men take it on to the mortuary. You going?"

"To the post-mortem. My super wants me there."

"Come and have some tea, then. You'll need it. If you think it's cold out here wait till you cop that place."

31

MILTON stood by the blackboard on which he had written "Male, white. Age approx. 22. Height 5' 9½". Weight 148 lbs." He had watched with some interest as the mortuary-keeper and his assistant had stripped the body and sluiced it free of mud. He had himself screwed down the rigitator on to the dead fingers and carried out the ritual of taking fingerprints.

He was conscious of a sickening knot in the stomach as the pathologist approached: a small man with a clerky face, somehow dreadful in his red rubber apron and boots. Beside the pathologist was a very tall and very thin medical student with an intense face. He carried, in a leather case hanging from a strap on his shoulder, a portable tape recorder. He held the microphone conveniently close to the pathologist. Milton saw the knife raised and turned away. He heard nothing, and after an unbearably long time his eyes returned to the table in time to see the pathologist raise a portion of the lower intestine on the end of a long probe. Milton turned away, but the image was engraved on his consciousness. He had a sudden desperate longing for a cigarette.

He was careful not to look towards the dissection table again, but he could not block his ears to the grating of the saw nor to the closing of the rib secateurs. Nor to the pathologist's dictation.

"Third and fourth ribs cracked, fifth rib fractured. Heavy bruising subcutaneous layers. Abrasion right dorsal, extensive bruising whole upper chest area." The pathologist's voice was completely without inflection. "Skin abrasion, incision approximately half-inch width, very deep, left groin, bruising left thigh."

And again. "Head bruised, small indention right temple. Raised area left jaw, heavy bruising, cracked cheekbone."

Milton leaned against the white tiled wall. He closed his eyes. The voice droned on. The river sergeant had been right, the mortuary was cold, but with a different, more insidious coldness than that of the river. Milton found himself thinking of Sally Carter, the antithesis of everything that was cold and bitter and dead. He deliberately tried to wrench his thoughts elsewhere, and concentrated on Brockhouse's grandfather. An old man, a fine old man, a creator who had lived his long life in tune with the mysterious rhythm of the earth itself. And now, at the very end of his life, bewildered by the severance of his line; before him nothing but the void, no youthful hand reaching forth to take up his gifts of life and fruits and peace. An old man looking calmly forward into nothing but darkness.

Aren't we all? thought Milton. Why is it that we live so badly? Why is it that we are all destroyers? He closed his eyes, and suddenly he was at the top of a scenic railway. It was an enormous height because he was only nine years old and he was being very brave about it. He had been looking forward to it all the week, but now, standing at the very front of the car, clinging desperately to the guard rail, he was afraid. He was going faster and faster; the wind was whipping through his hair, and he could not fully open his eyes. He was being buffeted this way and that. All the passing stanchions and girders were moving at bewildering speed. He shouted above the sound of the wind to show that he was enjoying himself, and to give the lie to the taste of bile at the back of his throat.

Milton opened his eyes. The pathologist had removed his apron and gloves and was washing his hands at the sink on the far wall. He finished by sluicing his hands in surgical alcohol, waving them in the air until they were dry. He looked tired.

He looked towards Milton. "The contents of the stomach

188

will be analysed in my laboratory, and when that has been done I will give my report in writing."

"I see."

"Not that there will be much doubt about it : almost all the injuries were caused prior to death. He was deeply unconscious when he entered the water, but he was not dead—that's obvious from the amount of water in the lungs. He would have died anyway; he would hardly have recovered from those injuries. To all intents and purposes he was beaten to death. The man who did it must have thought he was dead."

"Was there any sign of drugs?"

The pathologist shrugged. "No signs of puncture, but anything taken by mouth wouldn't show up here. It may when we analyse the stomach contents, but even then anything like amphetamine enters the bloodstream so quickly that traces would hardly be found. Either way, drugs would not have made much difference. This man was systematically beaten; very badly beaten indeed. He was a criminal?"

"Yes," said Milton.

The tall assistant was screwing down the lids of large glass bottles containing portions of organs. They had no effect on Milton, but he was careful not to look at the dissection table. He shook hands with the pathologist, and also, to his surprise, with the medical student.

Once he had left the mortuary he found himself engulfed by people. Now that he was no longer near the river the wind was not so biting. It was a very bright day, and the crowds that wound their way past him were on their way to lunch. He kept having to move to the edge of the pavement to avoid groups of young girls who huddled together in giggling conspiracies.

At the entrance to the Tube station he bought a midday edition paper from an old man with a club foot. It was a racing edition, and the front page was full of course correspondents' information. As his train rattled past Chancery Lane he came across an item on an inside page which reported the opening of a luxurious "supper casino" in Berkeley Square where Mr Howard Griffen, "well-known West End club-

189

owner", had welcomed celebrities with a champagne supper. There was a photograph of him in a dinner-jacket with eager-eyed "actresses" on either side of him of whom Milton had never heard. Milton grinned savagely, and the girl sitting opposite him uncrossed her legs and tucked her skirt firmly under her thighs.

As Milton closed his eyes she felt that she had won a small victory, but Milton was fast asleep.